A Gift of Ghosts

Sarah Wynde

Published by Rozelle Press
independent publisher of unexpected fiction
rozellepress.com

Cover design by Karri Klawiter, artbykarri.com
ISBN: 1470130270
ISBN-13: 978-1470130275

❧DEDICATION❧

A quirky dedication for a quirky book: this book is dedicated to the creators, cast, and crew of the (wonderful, amazing, incredibly fun, tragically cancelled) television show *Eureka*, for first inspiring my creativity and then annoying me so much that I was forced into originality.* And in particular, to Felicia Day, for this blog post: http://feliciaday.com/blog/five-things-about-2010, and for making geeky girls cool.

**Ahem. Or 95% originality? The Quirky Town trope isn't exactly new. Other superficial similarities and hidden allusions to Eureka are intended as homage.*

~CHAPTER ONE~

Akira checked her reflection in the sun visor mirror. She'd bitten off all her lipstick during the drive from the airport. Hands shaking, just a little, she pulled out a pink gloss from her bag and carefully reapplied the color.

"You're awfully pretty, you know." The teenage boy leaning over the back of the seat made the words sound disparaging. "It's not like you need that. It's probably going to give you cancer or something. Why do girls think it's a good idea to spread chemicals all over their faces?"

Ignoring him, she took a deep breath, and tucked the gloss back into the pocket of her bag, trying to summon up the courage to step out of the car. She'd walk into the building and breeze her way through her first job interview in years. She could do it. Of course she could. She'd be bright and smart and professional, and they'd love her and offer her a job, a good job, one that would let her actually work on her research.

"And then I'll win the lottery," she said aloud, chewing on her lip, already forgetting about the gloss.

"No one ever does," the boy said cynically.

Akira wasn't even sure how she'd made it here. She wasn't the adventurous type. Life, it seemed to her, had enough challenges without searching out new ones. She'd mapped out her path long ago: a nice, quiet academic life in the Californian town where she grew up, some teaching, some research, staying in familiar territory, living on familiar ground.

But then one reckless paragraph about spirit energy in an article for the prestigious Energy Research Quarterly, and suddenly all her plans were in jeopardy. The committee hadn't denied her tenure yet, but her department head had made it clear that it was only a matter of time. With no hope of a university job, she'd have to teach in a high school. She'd rather work in the fifth circle of hell.

The phone call from General Directions, Inc. had been out of the blue, but it felt like a potential lifesaver. The company wanted to meet with her. They were willing to fly her to Florida—Florida, of all places!—rent her a car, and put her up in a hotel room for a day or two, while they interviewed her for some undefined position.

Despite the vagueness of the details, Akira hadn't hesitated.

But she was hesitating now. She sighed. She couldn't sit in the car forever. Might as well go in and get it over with. She took one last glance in the mirror and for a quick second her eyes met those of the boy in the back seat.

"Hey," he said, pushing himself away from where he'd been leaning. "Hey, did you . . ."

Akira, though, was already out of the car, closing the door firmly behind her.

The brick buildings, lush grass, bright flowers, and flowing water in front of her were undeniably beautiful. But where was the research lab she'd been expecting? She'd pictured a square box, five stories high, with mirrored windows, set in the middle of a giant parking lot. The kind of place that could exist anywhere, neither fitting in nor standing out.

The kind of place where maybe she could exist without fitting in or standing out.

This looked more like an extremely exclusive private school.

She made her way up the cobblestone walkway to the front door of the nearest building. Although the friendly guard at the security booth way back up a winding road had told her that she'd found her destination, she still felt unsure of herself until a discreet sign on the wall labeled General Directions, Inc. reassured her that at least she was in the right place.

General Directions. The name was so very generic.

At the front desk, she introduced herself, trying not to let her uncertainty show. "Akira Malone, here for an interview."

"Of course." The young blonde woman behind the desk responded with a warm smile, her eyes just a little curious. "Mr. Latimer's been expecting you. I'll show you right in."

ॐ

Zane Latimer was playing his twentieth game of solitaire on a borrowed computer in a usually unused office. He liked his own office just fine. It was comfortable and cluttered and a great place for thinking. At least for him. His sisters claimed it was full of distractions.

But his office was too revealing for an interview like this one. The stark walls, empty desk, two metal chairs, ugly carpeting, and old desktop computer in this room presented a much better image for his purposes. He wondered if this candidate would notice the lack of a phone. There really ought to be a big clunky corded phone with square buttons. He made a mental note to search one out before the next interview.

He glanced at his watch again. His agent at the tiny private airport had called half an hour ago. Ms. Malone had arrived without incident, but had requested a different car immediately upon seeing the black Taurus that was waiting for her. With no other car available, she had reluctantly accepted the keys from the clerk. The clerk had reported this with interest: she was paid well to note the arriving guests' attitudes about their transportation, but this was the first time she'd had anything to say. Zane accepted the information without comment, but had been waiting a little more impatiently than usual ever since.

Ms. Malone was the fourth person he'd interviewed. As far as he was concerned, this job search was a wild goose chase. But his father had insisted, and when Max Latimer dug his heels in, people around him mostly sighed and acquiesced. Mostly.

Zane stood as Grace opened the door without knocking, and ushered the latest candidate inside. He paused, his mouth not quite dropping open. This—she—wasn't what he'd expected at all. Over Akira's dark head, his sister raised her eyebrows and grinned, and then gave him a hasty thumbs-up behind Akira's back.

"This is Zane Latimer," she said to Akira. "He'll be interviewing you today. Can I get you anything? Coffee, tea, some water?"

"I'm good, thank you," Akira responded, tugging at the edges of her black suit jacket and then extending her hand to Zane where he stood behind the desk. "How do you do, Mr. Latimer?" she asked with an old-fashioned formality.

"Ah, fine. And you?" he answered on auto-pilot, shooting a perplexed gaze at Grace. She shrugged as she pulled the door closed behind her, still grinning, and he gestured toward the uncomfortable chair on the other side of the desk.

"Quite well, thank you." Akira perched on the edge of the chair, holding her bag in front of her.

"How was your flight?" he asked as he took his own seat.

"This morning's?" she answered. "It was the smallest plane I've ever been on. It was interesting." Her lips curved in an almost smile.

Zane couldn't tell whether interesting meant white-knuckled terror or gazing out the window in delight. At Max's behest, General Directions had arranged for Akira to fly from California to central Florida on a commercial airliner the day before, staying in an airport hotel for the night. That flight was a standard commercial flight. This morning's much shorter hop was in a Piper Seneca, a six-seat twin-engine plane. Zane loved it, but it was not the type of corporate jet that featured flight attendants serving champagne, kitchens, fancy conference rooms and sofas.

Leaning back in his chair, Zane steepled his fingers together. He enjoyed interviewing, but for the first time, he wished he'd found out more about this applicant than her name. He'd grabbed a slim file folder from his father's desk when he came in this morning, but he hadn't bothered to open it. It was now sitting on the desktop in front of him.

"So, how did you hear about us?" he started.

"Uh, you called me?" Akira responded, sounding doubtful. "I don't know very much about the company. The man I spoke with on the phone last week told me you'd tell me more at the interview."

"I see." Zane leaned forward, touching the folder but not quite picking it up. "In that case, why don't you tell me a little about yourself?"

"I—do you mean—are you interested in my research? Or my teaching?" Akira stumbled to a halt.

Zane gave her a polite smile, trying not to let his confusion show. Max must have called her. But where had he found her? Research? Teaching? That didn't fit the usual profile. Max had been sorting applications and resumes for months, and this was only the fourth time he'd wanted to bring a candidate in for an interview. But Ms. Malone was completely unlike the others.

It wasn't that the first three had been similar physically, but they'd had a certain kind of gloss, a polished exterior, and a projected warmth that made their differences disappear. This one was a mouse.

A cute mouse. Maybe even an adorable mouse, like a chipmunk or a jerboa. Zane tried to think of other types of mice. Was there one with dark eyes and round cheeks and fluffy hair? That would be the right kind of mouse. Suddenly he realized that he'd let the pause drag on too long and that the mouse was looking increasingly nervous.

"Right, research, tell me about your research."

She sighed with obvious relief, and plunged into a description that within the first few words flew totally over Zane's head. "Sono—what?" he finally interrupted.

"Sonoluminescence. Specifically, stable single-bubble sonoluminescence. I've been experimenting with the noble gases—argon, xenon . . ."

Before she could continue, he put up one finger to pause her and flipped open the folder that was on the desk. The single sheet of paper inside wasn't a job application. Or even a resume. It was the last page of an academic article, with a red circle around the final paragraph.

"Potential energy?" he said out loud, skimming it quickly. "Ah, spirit energy."

Akira seemed to go a little paler, if that was even possible. "That's not . . . I mean that was simply a speculative, theoretical idea. Just a hypothetical possibility that might be—"

"What is it you do exactly?" Zane interrupted her, still puzzling over the article. "Energy Research Quarterly? What is this?"

"I'm a physics professor. I teach at Santa Marita College. In California?" Akira said it as a question.

"A physics professor?" Zane couldn't stop his lips from twitching, but he tried hard to swallow the smile. Okay, his father had gone around the bend. What in the world were they going to do with a physics professor? General Directions had a research division, but they tended to work more on biochemistry and medical projects. And Zane didn't hire the scientists.

A quiet tap at the door interrupted them and Akira looked back at it with relief. "Shall I—" she started as the door swung open behind her, and Grace entered holding another folder.

Grace looked at Zane, her eyes laughing. "I'm so sorry to interrupt," she said smoothly, "but Max wanted you to have this."

He took the folder she handed over with some relief. This must be the rest of the information about Ms. Malone. Enlightenment was at hand. He flipped the folder open.

Or not.

The folder contained three documents: General Direction's standard non-disclosure agreement; General Direction's standard employment contract, already filled out with Akira's information; and a sticky note that said "Natalya says yes. Give her whatever she wants, but get her to sign a two-year-contract." His father's illegible signature was scrawled across the bottom.

A two-year contract? That was ridiculous. The contracts used at General Directions were typically for short-term contract labor, three or six months at most. Why would Max want this woman to commit to such a long stay?

"Did he say anything else?" Zane asked Grace, not hiding his surprise.

"No, I'm afraid not."

"But . . ." He glanced at Akira. "Excuse us for just a minute."

Standing, he took Grace by the arm and ushered her into the hallway, pulling the door almost closed behind them. In an urgent whisper, he asked, "What job does he want me to give her? What exactly is she supposed to do for us?"

Grace shrugged.

"You're enjoying this, aren't you?"

"I love seeing you confused, darling." Grace patted his cheek. "She's not the usual type, is she?"

"Has Max lost his mind? She's a physics professor. I thought I was hiring a . . ." He glanced back at the door, realizing that Akira might be able to overhear them. "It's not like I interview every employee. Shouldn't Smithson be hiring the scientists?" he asked, naming the head of GD's research division.

Grace shrugged again.

"Well, is she supposed to work for special affairs or research or what?";

"You know as much as I do. I guess it's up to you."

"Okay." Zane sighed. Did he want the mouse working for him or not? Well, yes. A reluctant smile crossed his face.

Back in the office, he sat down behind the desk. She looked quite miserable. She had the kind of face, fluid and expressive, that would have been wonderful on a stage—even the audience in the farthest reaches of the theater would be able to see her emotions. But it might have been better for her if she'd been a better actress, more able to hide what she was feeling.

Zane had planned to continue asking her questions while he tried to figure out what to do with her, but he couldn't resist ending her misery. "So we'd like to offer you a job," he found himself saying. "You'll need to sign a two-year contract. And what's your current salary?"

"I—what?" she asked.

"Your current salary?" he repeated patiently.

She named a figure, but then added, "But wait . . ."

He added twenty-five percent to the number and said the new total out loud, then added, "And Florida is much less expensive than California. You'll find your standard of living quite different in Tassamara, I suspect."

"But wait," she said again. "What do you want me to do? What would the job entail?"

"Research." He smiled, probably a little too brightly, while he tried to figure out what the right answer to that question might be.

"But I don't even know what General Directions is. It's an extremely vague name. What does the company do?"

"Oh, a little bit of this, a little bit of that. Some government work, some private research, some investments in other companies."

She frowned at him, and he couldn't resist the urge to tease her a little. Quite solemnly, he said, "Nothing X-rated, of course," as if that was her paramount concern. Her eyes widened, and he tried not to smile, but a quiver of mischief escaped.

Narrowing her eyes, she forged forward, obviously determined to ignore his distractions. "My concern is the government work. Are you a defense contractor?"

"Do you have reason to believe you wouldn't get a security clearance?" he asked, interested now.

Again, she looked startled. "No, but I don't want my research used to make weapons."

This time he looked surprised. "Do you think that's likely?" He flipped open the folder again and looked at the minimal material inside. What exactly was her work?

"Well, I don't know." Her exasperation was clear. "I haven't completed it yet. I don't have any results. But I'd like some reassurance that if I do have any interesting findings, they won't be promptly locked up in a top-secret project for military use."

"I can assure you that we have never developed any weapons for the government. Any government."

"So what do you do for the government? Any government?" She repeated his phrasing pointedly, and he couldn't resist smiling at her. She didn't smile back, but for just a moment, a dimple appeared in her cheek.

"Oh, ah, well . . ."

"Don't tell me. A little of this, a little of that?"

"More or less."

"So you're offering me a job, but you don't want to tell me anything about what the company does, or what I would be doing?"

"Something like that."

She frowned, and he could see the indecision on her face, so he added, "I can tell you that you'll be free to pursue your own research. On sonoluminescence . . ." He stumbled over the name, then added, ". . . or whatever." He doubted she'd actually be researching that science stuff for long: Max must know something more than he was saying about what she was capable of.

She was still looking doubtful, so he slid the non-disclosure agreement across the desk to her. "Sign that, I'll give you a tour, we can talk about what kind of lab and equipment you need, and then you can decide."

He took out a pen and added the salary figure to the two-year contract, then showed it to her. "You will have to commit to two years. But there's no need to think about that until you've had your tour."

ँ

Akira took a deep breath before starting the car. She was not at all sure how she felt about this, but apparently she was going to move to Florida. She couldn't suppress a little glow of joy when she thought about the beautiful labs she'd seen. Even her uncertainty about why exactly she'd been hired couldn't dim her delight at the idea of uninterrupted time to do nothing but explore her ideas.

"You look happy," the boy in the back seat said. "Maybe you did win the lottery."

Akira didn't respond, but her happiness dimmed a little.

"I wonder who you saw in there. Let's see. Maybe I can figure out what you do. Maybe you were selling something? No. Maybe you're a librarian? No." The boy gloomily sank back into his seat and said, "This game's not much fun when I'll never know."

He looked out the window, and sighed. "Twenty-five minutes to the airport and then back to the parking lot."

Akira bit her lip. "So, what's your name?"

The boy's eyes widened and he leaned forward again. "You can see me!"

"Yeah, but don't get all excited about it."

"Are you kidding? I haven't spoken to anyone in months. I'm trapped in this car. I mostly sit in a parking lot. And you're living!"

"Again, don't get all excited." Akira knew exactly how this was going to go, and it wasn't going to be fun. She probably should have just kept pretending she didn't see him. But he'd looked so sad and she'd been so happy. She hadn't been able to stay cold to him.

"So, do you help me? Like, find a light or something?"

"That'd be nice, wouldn't it?" Her voice was dry. "No, unfortunately, I don't know anything about lights. And if you want me to go talk to any relatives—well, it never ends well. I'd really rather not."

"But isn't that what you do?"

"No, that's just how it works on television." Akira sighed and flipped her blinker on. The guard shack was just ahead, and she didn't want to be seen talking to herself.

"But . . . but you can see me!" She glanced back at him in the rear view mirror. Yes, she could see him, and he was quite a charmer, really. He must have been about fourteen or fifteen when he died, tall and gawky in that adolescent way, all arms and legs, with a shock of curly dark hair and intense blue eyes.

She pulled out onto the busy street, and with the guard safely behind her, asked again, "Do you have a name?"

"It's Dillon. You mean you really can't help me?"

She shook her head. "Not so much, no."

"Man, that bites." He flopped back against the seat again, looking disgusted. "I finally find someone who can see me, and she's useless. Um, no offense."

Akira bit back her smile. She didn't mind useless, actually. She'd heard worse. "I can listen," she offered. "And I know a little."

"Do you know why I'm stuck?" he asked. "I mean this can't happen to everyone. I met a guy at a gas station once, but it's not like the roads are crowded with us."

"Oh, there's a fair number of you on the highways, actually. It used to be quite a nightmare for me when I was first learning how to drive. I kept getting distracted. My dad would . . . never mind." She shook that thought away.

She glanced at her watch. "I don't have to be at that airport for the trip back to Orlando for about five hours. Where do you want to go?"

"You're serious?" he asked.

She nodded. "But no relatives, please." She looked pained. "Honestly, it never works out well."

ᘓ

She'd been given clear instructions on where to drop off the car, but as she drove up to the parking lot, she couldn't help worrying. Unlike the usual rental car experience, she'd been told she'd be met by someone who would collect the keys.

"So you remember what I told you, right?" she asked Dillon.

"Every word," he assured her.

"Work on stretching. I know the bounce-back is no fun, but if you practice, you'll find that you're able to get farther and farther away from the car. It's like exercise, it's going to be painful at first, but the rewards will be worth it."

"I will. Are you kidding? Being out of this car would be so great. I'll practice every day."

"And avoid the ghosts with the red edges. If you see someone who looks like they're outlined in red, go the other direction."

"I will," he promised, but this time with less enthusiasm.

"I'm serious. I know you're lonely and you probably think any company is better than none, but it's not. The red ghosts are bad news."

"I'm already dead. What can they do to me?"

"Oh, sweetie." She shook her head. "If you think boredom is the worst thing that can happen, then you didn't watch nearly enough television while you were alive. Trust me on this one." She turned and stared at him, eyes intent, knowing that she was probably the first person who'd looked directly at him since his death. "Stay away from ghosts with red edges."

He nodded.

"And stretch." She pointed a finger at him and smiled, and he smiled back, a mix of emotions fighting for precedence on his face.

She spotted someone approaching through the back window, and said hastily, "Gotta go. You take care."

Stepping out of the car, she greeted the young woman. As she handed over the keys, she impulsively said, "I'm going to be moving to this area in a few weeks and I'll need to lease a car. Is there any chance that this one might be available?"

The girl looked startled. She glanced from the car to Akira and back to the car again, before saying, "This car? But . . . um, well, I guess. I mean, I don't know. I can ask." Her tone was doubtful.

"That would be great," Akira said. "Do you have a number or something I could call when I get back?"

"Sure. Yeah. You could ask at GD. Ask Grace." The girl nodded, her uncertainty disappearing. "Grace will know. She'll be able to help you."

~CHAPTER TWO~

Akira had decided that Florida was creepy. She was beginning to doubt her decision to move here. Again. For only the hundredth time.

She hadn't even gotten out of the car at the first house Meredith, the realtor, had shown her, despite Meredith's protesting, "Oh, but it's a darling little house. Recently remodeled, fully updated inside, the latest appliances, and the rent is very reasonable."

Akira had just sighed and said, "It's not right for me." The cranky old woman ghost on the front porch had waved her fist at them as they drove away, although Akira was sure that the faint "good riddance" she heard was her imagination.

At the second house, Akira stopped at the bedroom door and swallowed hard. It was unfurnished, the walls freshly-painted a light off-white. Meredith strode in, talking about the adjoining bathroom as if the translucent weeping girl on the floor, holding a baby, and rocking back and forth, was invisible. Which, of course, she was—to the realtor. Suicide? Akira thought dispassionately. Maybe natural causes for the baby, and then mom's grief drove her to kill herself? Or perhaps a post-partum depression murder-suicide?

"Aren't you going to come look? It's really quite lovely." Meredith had a chirpy voice. Akira was beginning to dislike it.

"No, thank you," Akira said calmly. "I don't think it's right for me." Turning, she marched out of the house and straight to the car. By the time Meredith caught up, she was already seated and buckled in the passenger-side seat, staring straight ahead.

"You're going to fit right in around here," Meredith said, as she slid the key into the ignition and pulled away from the curb. Akira shot her a curious look. Now what did that mean?

Meredith smiled at her, a little wryly. "Now this next house is big for you, but it's in your price range, and Dr. Latimer suggested that you might be interested in it."

"Dr. Latimer? Is that Zane Latimer?"

"No, no, it was Max Latimer. He was the one who set up your appointment."

Akira frowned. She'd tried to research the company from California, but it was almost invisible. Oh, it had a web site, a completely unrevealing web site. The copywriter who wrote the text had been a master of saying nothing in many, many words. Apart from that, the name was too generic. The phrase "general directions" had 14 million hits on Google, most of them maps. Akira had deduced that the company was privately owned, but that was about as far as she'd gotten.

"I don't believe I met him," she told Meredith.

"No?" Meredith's voice was casual. She tucked a strand of long red hair behind one ear as she ostentatiously paid attention to traffic, of which there was none.

"Is there something I ought to know about him?" Akira asked, exasperated. She was getting a bit tired of the mystery. Over the course of the past month, she'd given notice at the college, rented out her house, packed up her belongings, putting some in storage and arranging for the rest to be shipped to Florida, said good-bye to everyone and everything she knew, and flown to Orlando.

This time there was no private plane to deliver her almost straight to General Directions, so she'd made the long, slow, winding drive north in a rental car. She'd gotten to Tassamara expecting to check into a hotel and start work immediately. Instead, Grace told her to take her time getting settled and introduced her to Meredith, a pretty mid-30s redhead who would "show her everything important." As far as Akira could tell, though, there was nothing important in Tassamara. She wasn't even sure she'd seen the town yet. It seemed to be a blink-and-you'll-miss-it spot on the map.

"Most of the people in Tassamara work for him either directly or indirectly," Meredith finally said. "GD is the only company in town."

"Which means what? He runs the place like an old-time mining town? What he says goes?"

"Oh, no, no," Meredith chuckled. "You'll like him, I'm sure. Everyone does. He's just . . . well, you'll see." She pulled to the side of the road and parked.

Akira didn't move to get out. "He's just what? Pick a word, any word. I've moved here all the way from California, I don't know anybody, and if I've made a huge mistake, then the sooner I figure it out, the better." She knew she was being too blunt, but she couldn't help herself.

Taking a job so far away from home had been an act of denying imagination: she'd convinced herself to do it by focusing on the lab and the work. She hadn't tried to picture what her life would be like, where she'd live or buy her groceries or go for walks, who her friends would be or what she'd do on weekends. She had very deliberately not thought about the challenges of navigating unfamiliar places, strange houses, unknown landscapes. If she had thought about all those things . . . well, she would have been working at the 7-11 down the street from her house in California and going hungry to pay the bills rather than braving all of this uncertainty.

It wasn't that she was a coward, she assured herself. But her challenges were different than those of most other people, and she had to be careful in a way that most people wouldn't understand. Okay, and maybe she was a little bit of a coward.

Meredith smiled at her. "Eccentric. Dr. Latimer is eccentric. But really, I think you're going to fit right in in Tassamara. It's a quirky little town." She gestured at the house behind Akira. "That's the place. You should take a look."

Quirky? Akira didn't feel better. But she turned and looked. The house was two stories, white frame, with a wraparound porch and a turret. She glanced back at Meredith in surprise. Was she kidding? "There's only me, you know. I'm not bringing a family."

Meredith was already getting out of the car. "Come take a look. Like I said, it's a little big, but Dr. Latimer thought you might like it."

Akira followed her up the short walkway. The house was close to the street, and she looked around curiously at the neighboring houses. "Are we near the town?"

"Yes, Millard Street is the main drag, and it's about two blocks that way. An easy walk, if you don't like to drive."

Akira didn't mind driving, although being able to walk for small errands would be pleasant. But the mention of driving reminded her of the black Taurus and Dillon. She'd asked Grace if she could lease the car that she'd driven the first day, with no idea what she'd answer when Grace asked why. After all, it was just an ordinary car, several years old, nothing special about it if you couldn't see the ghost boy inhabiting the back seat, and no reason to want that car rather than some nice new model.

But Grace hadn't asked why. She'd paused and her face had stilled, then she'd turned away and busied herself with some files, before turning back, smiling cheerfully, and saying, "I think that can be arranged. I'll have it waiting at the airport."

Akira still wasn't sure whether she'd seen something on Grace's face—sadness? worry?—or whether it had been her imagination. But she'd been too relieved that Grace hadn't asked her any hard questions to try to decipher Grace's response.

Meredith unlocked the door, gave a hard push, and shoved it open. "Door's a little sticky, we might need to get someone out to take care of that." She stepped into the house and Akira followed, feeling wary.

The first two rooms were empty and echoing. Hardwood floors were worn and battered, showing signs of hard use, and the fireplace in the front room was blackened with years of smoke. But the light was nice and the ceilings were high, with overhead fans. A narrow staircase led upstairs to a hallway that extended in both directions. Another hallway led to the back of the house.

Meredith chatted about paint colors and furniture, but Akira wasn't really listening. She turned slowly, looking around. The house had a feeling. But not a bad feeling. It should have felt abandoned, alone, the way houses that were uninhabited always did. But this house, despite its emptiness, felt lively. Akira's wariness increased. Was this town simply infested with ghosts?

She followed Meredith down the hallway, passing a small bathroom, and into the kitchen.

"Rose! We have visitors." An old man was folding his newspaper and standing up as Akira walked into the room. She glanced quickly at Meredith. No reaction. Okay, so he was a ghost. Akira kept her eyes off him, not wanting him to realize she could see him, but she tried to steal looks from the corner of her eye, as she murmured something in response to Meredith's running commentary.

He looked like a kindly grandpa. Not her kindly grandpa—she'd never met any of her grandparents—but like a television version of a kindly grandpa, with white hair and laugh lines and a little more belly than had probably been good for him. He was wearing what she thought of as golf clothes: a collared, short-sleeved shirt, with a sweater vest, and plain light-colored pants.

"Oh, yay!" A whirlwind came barreling through a doorway that

Akira hadn't noticed and she had to concentrate hard on Meredith's face to keep from staring openly. The young woman clapped her hands, and twirled in the center of the room, her peach skirts flaring around her. "Maybe she'll get cable. Maybe she'll love that music show. Quick, what can we do to keep her? I know, let's make it smell like chocolate-chip cookies."

The old man chuckled. "Now there's a nice idea. You'll have to work on that. It'd be right pleasant if you could make that happen."

"Oh, I do hope she stays. Should we call the boys in?" Rose danced her way to the back door, within Akira's line of sight, and pressed against it, peering out the window. Tall, willowy, with long blond curls, she was dressed in the full skirts and sleeveless top of the 1950s.

"Now, Rose, you know it's been ages since they've come inside. You leave them be. They're fine."

Rose turned and Akira hastily directed her attention to Meredith. "I'm sorry, what were you saying?"

Meredith was watching her, a curious look on her face. "Some people think this house is haunted." She made the statement calmly, almost casually, without even a hint of thrill in her voice.

"Noooo!" Rose wailed. "Don't do that. You'll scare her off."

"Oh, dear, that's bad," the old man murmured. "That must be why we've been empty for so long."

"It was that last lady, the one who lit that smelly stuff, and tried to talk to us. But she couldn't hear a thing." Rose actually stamped her foot.

"They say the ghosts are friendly, though." Meredith was smiling, but her look was too intent, too expectant.

"We are, we are friendly," Rose burst out. "We like people. Oh, please live here. I miss television. I miss music. It's just too quiet without people."

"And do you believe in friendly ghosts?" Akira tried to infuse her tone with skepticism.

"In Tassamara, believing in six impossible things before breakfast is taken for granted. But let's move on. As you can see, the kitchen is nice, nothing special, but a good layout. The appliances all stay, including the refrigerator, and there's a washer and dryer over here in what used to be the pantry." Meredith opened the back door and stepped outside. "The back yard is fully enclosed and spacious for this area of town. There's a small pool and maintenance is included in the rent."

Akira followed her, but she was still puzzling over Meredith's first words. What impossible things? But as she looked out into the backyard, her thoughts derailed.

It was a pocket paradise. Flowering plants and lush bushes created a scenic border to a small yard where an oval pool, surrounded by brick pavers, played center stage. Two ghost boys ran and played as if the pool didn't exist.

They were the kind of ghosts that Akira thought of as faders. Unlike the ghosts in the kitchen, the boys were translucent to her, their colors dimmed and pale. But she could hear their laughter, and she couldn't help but smile in response.

"This is beautiful."

"Two citrus trees. You'll love the smell of the orange blossoms in another few weeks and the fruit would be yours, of course. Let me show you the upstairs." Meredith had reverted to a business-like realtor mode, and as Akira followed her back into the house and up the back staircase, she wondered what the realtor was thinking.

Upstairs, Meredith paused at the first door. "Four bedrooms, so as I said, it's big but you'll be able to pick which one you like and perhaps use another as an office. And lots of storage, of course. The rent is very reasonable, despite the size."

"That one's mine." Akira didn't react to the sound of Rose's voice behind her, just pasted a smile on her face for Meredith's benefit. "But you can share it, if you like. I wouldn't mind having a roommate. Oh, and if you like television at night, that would be so terrific. I promise I wouldn't talk much."

Akira glanced in the room. It was bright and big, but she kept walking. The next room was smaller and must have once been a child's room. She skipped that, too.

"Henry mostly stays downstairs, so you don't have to worry about him." Rose's tone was a little plaintive, as Akira opened the door to the turret room and stepped inside.

She crossed to the window and looked out, more to hide her face from the seemingly perceptive Meredith while she thought than to admire the view.

As a matter of principle, Akira avoided ghosts. She knew from painful experience that her interactions with them were hazardous.

But these ghosts weren't the dangerous kind: Rose had said they were friendly, but Akira hadn't needed her words. She could recognize a dangerous spirit from a distance, sometimes even from just a vibration in the air.

Of course, any ghost could become dangerous. And if her father knew she was even considering the idea of living with ghosts . . . but she didn't need to worry about his reaction, not anymore.

And then there was Dillon. Talking to him had been an impulse. When he sighed and mentioned the parking lot, she'd guessed he was tied to the car. That meant safety for her: he wouldn't be able to follow her home. He wouldn't be showing up in her bedroom or her shower or her classroom, like the ghost she'd spoken with back when she was a teenager who'd proceeded to make her life a living hell for months out of his own loneliness and misery.

She'd taken the risk, thinking it was for an afternoon, but she'd liked him. They'd fallen into conversation as easily as if they were old friends, talking about astronomy and science and movies and Harry Potter. Like most ghosts, he seemed desperately lonely but he was also curious and interested in the world. And he'd been willing to accept that she didn't have any answers for him.

Now she'd taken an even bigger risk by leasing the car. But bringing him here, to this house, might be good for him. He'd have at least two other ghosts to talk to, maybe more if the faders in the backyard weren't too far gone. It wouldn't be like life, of course, and every time she drove to work he'd have to come with her, but he'd have company.

Decision made, she turned back to Meredith. "I'll take it."

"You—? Okay. I'll arrange for the paperwork." Meredith looked a little surprised, although pleased, but her reaction was nothing compared to that of Rose who screamed with joy, and rushed away, yelling, "Henry, Henry, she's moving in."

"My office is on Millard. Why don't we go down there and you can take a look at the town while I get the lease together?"

"That sounds good." Akira looked around the turret room and smiled. Okay, her reasoning was logical. Scientifically sound. But she could also admit to herself that living in a turret would be a childhood dream come true.

On Millard Street, Akira strolled while Meredith drew up the paperwork, finally returning and sitting on a bench outside the realtor's office. The main street had a block with the usual shops: a gas station, with convenience store attached, a grocery store with a row of parking out front, even a small hardware store. A restaurant that hovered somewhere between being a café and a diner sat next to a small bookstore, an antique shop, and a store that looked as if it sold nothing but crystals.

She hadn't kept walking because the shops seemed to end and the buildings mostly became houses or small office fronts, lawyers and accountants, and perhaps the occasional doctor or dentist. It all seemed very typical. But there was something off about it. It was like a tourist town, but smaller, dustier, not as brightly colored or as artificially friendly. How did the town survive?

"My, what a beautiful aura you have, my dear." Akira automatically glanced in the direction of the voice, but then looked away, hoping the ghost wouldn't think anything of her response. A small woman—smaller even than Akira herself—dressed in a flowered muumuu had stopped and was staring at Akira. "It's lovely. Why, that blue is almost iridescent. I don't know that I've ever seen such a shade before. Do you have an unusual gift, child?"

"Hello, Mrs. Swanson." Meredith had opened the door to the realtor's office and Akira stood, surprised. So the little woman wasn't a ghost?

"Hello, Meredith, dear. How's your mother doing? I've been meaning to stop by."

"Oh, she'd be delighted to see you. She's been a little better lately, but she always likes to hear what's going on in town."

"Have you noticed your friend's aura? It's really quite remarkable." The little woman reached out as if to stroke Akira, but instead patted the air near her arm. Akira shifted, uncomfortable, but not wanting to be too obvious about her retreat. She threw a desperate look at Meredith but the realtor was smiling.

"What does it tell you?"

"Why, I'm not even sure. I was just asking her if she had a gift. I don't believe I've ever seen an aura like this before."

"This is Akira Malone. Akira, Mrs. Swanson, one of the long-time residents of Tassamara. She owns a small business a few blocks down. Akira's a new scientist with GD, Mrs. Swanson. I've just been showing her houses, and she's rented the old Harris place."

"A scientist? Well, that just seems wrong. But it's a pleasure to meet you, child." The woman reached out and took Akira's hand in both of her own, clasping it in an almost handshake, while gazing at the air around Akira's head.

"I, um, likewise, I'm sure," Akira mumbled, trying to retrieve her hand and succeeding.

"Akira needs to come in and sign her lease now, Mrs. Swanson, so we'll see you later." Meredith waved and Akira nodded a good-bye as she entered the realtor's office.

"Is she—was that—what does she do?" Akira asked. Was there a polite way to find out if Mrs. Swanson always accosted strangers on the street?

Meredith walked around to the other side of her desk and took her seat. "She's an aura reader, of course."

"A what?"

"She reads auras." Meredith said the words matter-of-factly.

Akira looked out the window at the departing back of the tiny woman and then at Meredith. "Are you serious?" Akira asked, as she sat in the chair in front of Meredith's desk.

Meredith looked surprised. "Of course. We're no Cassadaga, but Tassamara is a town of psychics. That does make us a bit unusual."

"A town of what?"

"Psychics. Cassadaga, of course, is famous for their spiritualists. We're much more private here." She leaned forward, lowering her voice, and added, as if confidentially, "I think we have more of the truly gifted here, too, but I shouldn't really judge."

Akira's face felt frozen. Meredith pushed the lease across the desk to Akira and dropped the keys on top of it, smiling.

For a moment, Akira paused. What had she gotten herself into? But, biting her lip, she picked up a pen and signed the lease, then scooped up the keys.

This town might be crazy.

But then, she might be crazy, too.

CHAPTER THREE

The black car was empty. Akira was surprised by the stab of disappointment she felt. Ghosts disappeared, she knew that. She had never known what exactly happened to them, but one day they'd be there, the next they were gone.

As a physicist, she'd theorized, although—with the exception of that one academic-career-destroying paragraph in the Energy Review Quarterly—only privately, never publicly. Were the spirits just a form of energy? Did it dissipate slowly for some, the faders, and burn out quickly for others? Or did it change? The first law of thermodynamics said that energy could neither be created nor destroyed, just transformed, so did spirit energy become some other form of energy? And if so, what?

But at the moment, the only important question was that she'd just leased an old black Taurus for no real reason, and did she want to keep it? She glanced back at the small airport building. She'd picked up the keys at the desk, and dropped off the keys to her rental car, as Grace had told her to do. She supposed she could go back in and say that she'd changed her mind, but that might be just as hard to explain as wanting the car in the first place could have been. She might as well just keep it.

She slid behind the wheel and adjusted the seat, and then the mirrors. Whoever had driven it out here had been a lot taller than she was. Set to go, she slid the key in the ignition, backed out of the parking space, and started to drive away.

The scream was piercing in its intensity, terrifying in its volume.

Akira slammed on the brakes, throwing the car into a skid. A flash of white, a loud bang, and suddenly the car was filling with smoke.

The next thing she was aware of was the feel of a strong, warm hand on her back as she tried hard to cough out her lungs to the sound of a teenage boy's voice saying, "I'm so sorry, I'm so sorry," over and over again.

"Just relax and try to breathe." That was an older, but also familiar male voice. Akira looked up. For a moment, she didn't recognize the face—it was too unexpected. But the dark hair, the blue-gray eyes—finally the pieces fell into place and she realized it was Zane Latimer, her erstwhile interviewer. "I'm calling an ambulance," he continued.

Frantically, Akira started shaking her head, while also trying to wave off Dillon's apologies. Through coughs, she gasped out, "No ambulance. No."

"Uh, yes, ambulance, yes," said Zane. "You were unconscious. I had to pull you out of the car because of the dust from the airbag. God knows what damage I might have done."

Through the coughing, through the pain that she was just starting to feel, Akira had room to feel a little burst of fear. Ambulances led to hospitals, and hospitals were bad. Very bad.

She was sitting on the gravel of the parking lot, she realized. Zane was crouched next to her, his hand on her back, and she was leaning against his legs. Dillon was on her other side. He'd stopped apologizing when she spoke, but he had his fist pressed against his mouth, his face frantic with worry.

She tried to smile at him, but it probably looked more like a grimace. It hurt to breathe. She thought that was just from the coughing, although she could tell that she would be bruised from the seat belt. And her arms hurt, too—long marks along the inside of her wrists were almost like brush burns, scraped and raw from the airbag's impact.

"I'll be okay." The words sounded strangled but she got them out.

"You were unconscious," Zane repeated. "I'm no doctor, but I know enough to know that unconscious is bad. You need to get looked at."

"I'm fine," Akira insisted. "It was just the airbag. I wasn't going very fast. What did I hit?" She tried to stand, pushing herself up with one hand. Zane slid his arm under her elbow and helped her to her feet, rising with a smooth, unconscious grace that she couldn't match.

"Looks like a parking post. You didn't do much damage, only dented the fender. It's too bad about the airbags, though. Cleaning up after a blown airbag is expensive. And it's an old car, and not worth much. The insurance company will probably want to total it."

"Total it?" Akira looked at Zane in dismay.

Standing by the car, Dillon's eyes went wide, and he put a possessive hand on the hood. "What will happen to me?"

Akira started shaking her head, "No, no, there's no need to call the insurance company. I'll get it repaired."

Zane's eyes narrowed. "You seem determined to keep this car."

Akira paused. She glanced at Dillon, and bit her lip, then looked away. What could she say? She coughed gently a few times, a delaying tactic as she tried to think things through. Should she let the car get totaled? Taken away to some junkyard? Stripped for parts, and then crushed? What would happen to Dillon?

If her father were here . . . but he wasn't. He'd been dead for three years.

Chin set stubbornly, she said, "I am, yes. I'll get the car fixed."

"Tell you what," Zane offered. "You let me take you to the hospital and have a doctor take a look at you, and I'll see about getting the car repaired."

Akira shook her head again. "No hospitals. I don't—I don't do hospitals."

"How can you not do hospitals? You're hurt. You could have internal injuries, a concussion, brain damage for all I know."

"I'm fine." The wince as she touched her chest probably didn't help convince him, but she did think she was fine, just bruised.

"I'm your boss. I could order you to go to the hospital," Zane suggested, exasperated.

Akira just looked at him. Obeying orders to go to the hospital was not in her job description. It was a vague job description, but if it entailed hospital visits, she was not going to be sticking around, contract or no contract. And while he might technically be her boss she was going to have a hard time thinking of him that way. Even in the formal interview setting, he had a casual air about him that said he'd rather be having fun than working, and today, in his blue jeans and t-shirt, he wasn't a convincing authority figure.

"Yeah, I didn't think that would work." Zane scratched his head. "What about this—my sister is a doctor and GD has a medical lab with all the latest scanners. Will you let her take a look at you?"

Akira thought about it, and then nodded. Medical care wasn't the problem. She just didn't like hospitals.

"All right." He took her chin between two fingers and tilted her head up. She met his gaze, surprised to feel a tingle of warmth touching her cheeks. What was he doing? Her lips parted slightly, almost involuntarily, as she realized how attractive he was. She hadn't thought of him that way, but standing so close to him, with his arms almost around her, his eyes intent on hers, she couldn't help but notice. "Your pupils are both the same size. That's about the only thing I know how to look for."

She pulled away. "I don't have a concussion."

"I'm going to call Nat and get her to meet us at GD. Will you wait here?"

Akira's confusion must have shown.

"I drove this car here," he said, nodding toward the black Taurus. "I was going to have a flying lesson, so my ride home won't be ready for a while. I'll see if I can clean this up enough to be drivable. Or at least enough to get us to GD."

"Oh, you know, if you have something to do, I'll be okay—" Akira started.

"Nice try." He brushed a finger along her cheekbone. "Wait here," he ordered. "I'll be right back."

Akira leaned back against the hood of the car. As Zane strode away, Dillon spoke, "I'm so sorry. I was working on stretching. I was in the hangar. But when the car started moving, it really hurt. I didn't realize what was happening."

"It's okay," Akira spoke quietly, watching for anyone who might be looking at them. "I'm sorry I messed up your car."

"What do you think would happen to me if the car got totaled?" asked Dillon, his tone fascinated yet uncertain.

"I think you'd be living in a junkyard," Akira answered. "I never have figured out how and why ghosts are tied to places, though. And with a car—well, I don't know. It might depend what you're really tied to. If it's the cushions or the spark plugs or the lights—maybe you'd move on with a part of the car?"

"Wow, that's a whacked idea. That'd be really strange. Stranger even than being a ghost in the first place."

"Kind of, yeah. Good thing you don't have to worry about it."

"It might be handy, though." Now that Dillon didn't have to be afraid, either for her or for himself, he was getting cheerful. "Just think, if I was tied to a spark plug, you could put it someplace cooler. Like maybe an arcade or something. Or a movie theater. I wouldn't mind haunting a movie theater."

Akira grinned at him. "Well, maybe we can experiment. But I think I've found us someplace to live that you're going to like."

"Someplace to live?" Dillon's face stilled. "Are you—" He stopped and Akira could see in his expression all of the loneliness and misery he'd been feeling, alone, trapped in a car, no one to talk to, for months or maybe years. Just the possibility of change had him frozen with doubt. She felt a wave of sympathy for him. She knew what it was like to be lonely, to not have anyone to talk to.

"I've leased the car, so you'll be staying with me." Akira tried not to get involved with the ghosts she saw. But Dillon was different. Maybe she couldn't find him a white light or fix whatever had made him a ghost in the first place, but she could make sure that his car was someplace nicer than a parking lot. "We're going to have to have some ground rules, though."

"No more parking lot?"

"No." Akira shook her head, but she couldn't help smiling at the look on his face. "And like I said, I think you're going to like the place I found for us to live. If you've been able to stretch enough to get into the hangar here, you'll definitely be able to get into the house. You might even be able to reach the town's main street, which could be fun, although what a weird little place that is. But—oh, hey, first rule." She turned so that she was facing away from the quickly approaching Zane. "Don't ever talk to me when people are around. Never, okay? It gets too confusing for me," she whispered.

"Okay, I won't. But thank you, thank you, thank you. You are the coolest person ever. You are the best. You—" Dillon put his hand over his mouth, as if to stop himself from talking.

Akira tried hard to stop smiling and look as if she was inspecting the car but Dillon's expression was so joyful that it was tough not to respond to it.

"Still feeling okay?" Zane asked from behind her.

"Uh-huh." She nodded, not looking at him.

"Dave lent me the portable vac, so I'll just cut out the airbag and clean up some of this powder. It'll take me maybe ten minutes. Do you want to go inside and sit down?"

"No, I'm good." Akira finally turned to face Zane, hoping she'd gotten her expression under control. He paused for a moment, looking at her intently, and then continued with his work, running the hand-held vacuum cleaner over the powdered seats and interior of the car. He was frowning, his face thoughtful.

Akira looked back at Dillon, who was hugging himself with

delight. She pressed her lips together, trying to stop herself from smiling, but she knew her eyes were giving her away. She glanced at Zane. He was watching her surreptitiously, and looked back at the car as soon as she looked at him, but fortunately, the vacuum cleaner was loud enough that there was no possibility of talking.

Within a few minutes, the car was cleaned to Zane's satisfaction, and the two of them were driving away. Or rather, the three of them, Dillon in the backseat, still quiet but almost glowing with happiness.

Zane glanced at Akira as they exited the parking lot, more successfully this time. He was driving. "How would you like to play twenty questions?"

"Animal, vegetable, mineral?" she responded, her voice skeptical.

"Maybe question ping-pong would be a better name. I ask you a question, you answer; you ask me a question, I answer."

Akira considered the idea. She wanted to know more about General Directions, about the eccentric Max Latimer, about Tassamara, but did she want to answer his questions? Zane was bound to ask her about the car and what could she say?

"For example," he went on. "This car. You obviously like it. But aren't you curious about it? Where it came from? Who owns it? Why it was the only car available to you on your first visit here?" With that, he had her hooked. He might ask her about the car, but yes, she had questions, too.

"All right. But I get to go first. Why was this the only car available?"

Zane grinned at her. "It was a test. My turn. Why do you want to keep it?"

"A test? But that's not an answer," Akira protested.

"Sure it is. Why do you want to keep it?"

"Sentimental reasons. What kind of a test?"

"A test of potential perception. Are you always sentimental about cars you drive once?"

"No." Potential perception? Akira's forehead creased with doubt. "Did I pass the test?"

"Oh, with flying colors, I think. You were the only candidate who expressed any reluctance to take the car. That's why it's so interesting that you want to keep it now." Zane paused. The first few rounds of their question ping-pong had been like a speed match, questions and answers flying. He tapped his long fingers on the steering wheel.

Akira frowned and glanced over her shoulder at the back seat. Dillon was leaning forward, looking curious. He opened his mouth as if to say something and she shook her head, very slightly, to tell him no. Carrying on two conversations at once was risky.

"Why were you reluctant to take the car?" Zane finally asked, taking his eyes off the road to watch her answer.

"I—" Akira didn't want to answer that question. What could she say after all? Maybe it was time to change the subject. "—am just very perceptive, I guess. Why did you offer me a job?"

"My sister, Natalya, the doctor that we're going to see, she said to hire you."

"But I didn't even meet her."

"That better not be a question. It's my turn."

"It's not a question, it's a statement. How could she—"

"Now that's sounding like a question," Zane interrupted. "It's still my turn. You have to wait for yours. Didn't you learn how to take turns in kindergarten?"

"Yes, I did. And you just used your question on that." Akira's tone was grumpy, but Zane laughed.

They were driving along the same narrow, winding road that Akira had taken the first time she'd been here. Oak trees draped in Spanish moss lined the sides of the road, making a dappled pattern of sun and shade on the asphalt. To Akira, used to the dry brown hills and open spaces of California, the sense of stillness and enclosed space felt mysterious, yet appealing. It was green and beautiful and wild.

But it was also strange.

She thought carefully before asking her next question. "Why did your father ask me to come here?"

"Ah, that's a good one. My father has been searching for a medium for a while now. He thought you might be one."

"A medium? You mean like a person who talks to dead people?" Horrified, Akira leaned toward Zane but then fell back as her seat belt pressed against her darkening bruises. "Ouch. What made him think that?"

"Not your turn." Zane's glance was worried. "You're not going to start coughing blood, are you?"

"No, I'm just bruised. What made your father think I was a medium?"

Zane turned onto the road that led to General Directions, slowing at the guard shack, but only pausing for a quick wave before the guard opened the gate. "My father likes to call himself a serendipidist. He's very good at putting random pieces of information together, and apparently that article you wrote struck him as intriguing. Intriguing enough to invite you out here."

"I can't talk to the dead," Akira said fiercely. The occasional dead person, okay, but only those who became ghosts. But most people just died. Her mother hadn't been a ghost. Her father hadn't been a ghost. Sometimes she still thought that she was insane and her ghosts hallucinations. Maybe she was simply a very competent schizophrenic.

"I'm pretty sure I'm dead. It took me a while to figure it out but it's the only thing that makes sense," Dillon spoke from the backseat and Akira glared at him, widening her eyes as if to tell him he was breaking the rules. This was not a time where she could afford to be confused. "Sorry," he added, falling back against the seat again, and pantomiming pulling a zipper across his lips.

"Hmm." Zane made a non-committal hum, and Akira gritted her teeth in frustration. "I'm not sure talking to the dead is all that uncommon. Anyone can do that. It's having the dead talk back that's unusual."

Zane pulled into a parking place and stopped the car, turning to face Akira. Very gently, he asked, "Do the dead talk to you, Akira Malone?"

"No! Not—" Akira looked away, not wanting to lie to him, and not wanting to tell him the truth, either, but unable to meet the searching look in his eyes.

"My nephew died in this car," Zane said.

The words were so random, so unexpected, that Akira's gaze flew back to his and before she thought, she blurted out, "Dillon's your nephew?"

Zane just looked at her. In the backseat, Dillon said dryly, "Dead giveaway. Excuse the pun. Tell Uncle Zane I say hi."

"Yes. My turn again." Zane's voice was still gentle. "How do you know my nephew's name?"

Akira looked away, trying to decide what to do. What had Meredith said? That Tassamara was a town of psychics? Maybe this was a place where it was safe to admit the truth. And maybe she had no choice, anyway, because it was too late not to.

"The dead don't talk to me," Akira admitted with reluctance. "Just ghosts. Ghosts talk to me." She sighed, and then added, mouth twisting, "But I talk back as little as possible."

☙CHAPTER FOUR❧

"Wow." It was more of a low sigh than an exclamation, as Zane shook his head. "Wow."

Akira waited, chewing on her lower lip.

People reacted differently to learning that she saw ghosts. Scoffing, disbelief, skepticism, she didn't really mind any of those: a quick, light, "Oh, of course I was kidding," and the conversation was over. Crazy manic enthusiasm and excitement? That happened sometimes and it was okay. Her best friend from childhood had loved her ghost stories, at least until her parents had talked to Akira's father. Absently, still watching Zane, Akira rubbed her lower arm.

Best-case scenario was what had happened with Mrs. Sato, her across-the-street neighbor when she was ten. She'd spent months being fussed over and fed home-made cookies with tall glasses of milk, while she provided a voice for the old woman's dead husband, until the day that Mrs. Sato didn't answer the door. She'd died in her sleep, and Akira had never seen either Mr. or Mrs. Sato again.

The worst-case scenario, though—that was bad. And it was always the relatives that were the worst. For some people, knowing a loved one was present but out of reach was devastating. Akira had never found the words that could make the loss bearable or the death meaningful.

"Would you mind telling Dillon that if he wasn't dead, I would kill him for being so stupid?" Zane finally said calmly.

The relief was like a cool breeze on a hot day. Akira had to bite back her smile.

"Ha!" Dillon said from the backseat. "At last I get to answer. Would you tell my uncle that he's said that every single time he's driven this car for years? I know already!"

"He can hear you," Akira replied to Zane.

"Oh." He glanced at her. "Right." He shook his head. "Wow," he repeated.

He looked back at her, more intently this time. "You—" he

started and then he stopped. "We need to get you checked out. Let's do that first. Dillon's not going anywhere, right?"

Akira looked at Dillon and shrugged. She never knew how or when a ghost would disappear.

"Yeah, go make sure you're not hurt," Dillon said. "I'll be fine. And not to be selfish or anything, but it'd suck big-time for me if you were to die right now."

This time Akira didn't bother to try to hide her wry smile. "That'd be ironic, wouldn't it? But I'm not badly hurt, I promise."

Zane's brow quirked, and Akira realized that she'd responded to words he couldn't hear. Quickly, she said, "Dillon agrees I should get looked at." Argh, she'd slipped already. Despite Zane's seemingly calm acceptance of a ghostly nephew, she'd learned that it was better, safer, to be careful.

Inside the General Directions building, Zane took her through an innocuous, unlabeled door behind the reception desk and into a small security room where a guard was watching multiple monitors. The guard acknowledged Zane with a laconic nod, but his alert eyes took in everything about Akira as they passed through the room, and into a hallway that led to an elevator.

This was such a strange place. That guard had the lean musculature and clipped hair of a professional soldier, and the wall of monitors was as high-tech as any security she'd ever seen. Research labs had security, of course, but this one was in the middle of nowhere. And it was a Sunday. Did they really need such precautions? And if so, why?

But as the elevator door slid open, she stopped worrying about it. The woman waiting on the other side had to be Zane's sister: she had the same dark hair, only hers was long and braided, and the same blue-gray eyes and fair skin. But where Zane had a look of hidden mischief, Natalya had a look of hidden depths, as if she had the kind of serenity that would be the calm in the midst of disaster, the still presence in a panicked emergency room.

"So Dad was right," Zane said, by way of greeting.

Natalya's eyes widened. "Dillon?" she asked.

Akira's eyes widened, too. If she'd known Zane was going to be so cavalier with her secret, she wouldn't have told him! Except, of course, that she'd given it away, she corrected herself. Still, she would have at least tried to swear him to secrecy before admitting the truth.

"Yep." Zane nodded. He looked back at Akira. "Is he here?"

"I—um—ah," Akira stammered a little, trying to decide what she should say, how she should answer, before admitting defeat, and saying, "No. He's tied to the car. He can't get this far away from it."

Natalya's mouth dropped open but only slightly, before she pulled it closed again and said, "Ghosts are real. And they haunt cars?"

Akira scowled at Zane, before shrugging reluctantly.

"And my nephew is a ghost?"

Akira's scowl deepened. Damn him for putting her into this position. She didn't do this! She didn't talk to relatives of ghosts. It just made for messy, uncomfortable scenes when Akira admitted that she didn't know why Dillon was a ghost, or how to help him, or really anything at all. Relatives always expected her to have the answers, as if seeing ghosts came with some gigantic book of profound insight into the spirit world. It didn't. Or if it did, her copy of the book had gotten lost in the mail.

"And Dad was right?" That final question wasn't directed at Akira, but at Zane, who was grinning.

"We should have known better than to bet against him," he acknowledged.

"That was you," Natalya said. "I did know better. And I look forward to Thanksgiving dinner. You'd better start practicing."

Maybe Akira was looking confused, because Zane took a moment to explain as they walked down the hallway. "A couple of years ago, my dad met a woman who claimed to be a medium. She told him that the car was haunted. He's been searching for another medium ever since. I bet him a home-cooked Thanksgiving dinner that she was lying, but he insisted that she was telling the truth. He's not usually wrong, so betting against him was probably not one of my better moves."

As they entered an examining room, Natalya shooed her brother away, sending him to another door further down the hallway. "We're not really a hospital," she explained. "I've got a medical degree, but I spend most of my time on research. I wouldn't have agreed to this, but Zane said you didn't think you were badly injured and our scanner is so much better than anything any local hospital has that if you do have any minor internal bleeding, I'm more likely to find it. We're using susceptibility weighted imaging, with a 3T high-field system, and the contrast is great for traumatic injuries." Clucking disapprovingly at the long scrapes on Akira's arms, Natalya handed her a flowered hospital gown.

Akira was mystified.

No one responded to the news that ghosts were real like this. It was as if Natalya had heard the words, accepted them immediately, and moved on just as quickly.

Where were the questions? The doubts? The demands for proof?

Natalya must have mistaken her surprise for lack of interest, because she continued with a smile, "Okay, I can see that you don't really care about my treasure. I'll skip the tech notes. Just take everything off, especially anything metal, and put the gown on. There's nothing metal in your body, is there? No pacemaker or artificial joints?"

Akira shook her head no, and Natalya went on. "The scanner is next door, and I'll be in the screening room on the other side with Zane. Just come through when you're ready, and lay down on the table. I'll be in to help you get comfortable." With that, she disappeared through the door.

Slowly, Akira changed into the gown, folding her clothes neatly and leaving them on the chair.

Maybe she had hit her head really hard.

Maybe she was dreaming?

But no, the scrapes on her arms hurt like hell, in the way that only brush burns and paper cuts could, a stinging pain of raw nerve ends. There was no way she was imagining that.

The table was cold but Akira was so busy thinking that she barely noticed as the machine whirred its way around her. The brief period where she and Zane had talked in the car had only added to her list of questions. She had been trying to hide her insanity for as long as she could remember, but everyone she'd met in this town seemed to be willing to accept it as matter-of-factly as if she'd told them the sky was blue. What was wrong with them?

❧

In the screening room, Natalya watched as images appeared on a computer screen, slide after slide showing sections of Akira's body. Zane, on the other hand, was watching the soles of Akira's feet through the glass. She had nice feet. Not that he could really see much of them from where he was standing, but they looked nice, narrow and pale.

"Ouch," Natalya said in a low voice, shaking her head as she stared at the monitor.

"Is she okay?" Zane asked, promptly turning his attention back to the computer screen. The images were just gray and white shapes: he had no idea what he was seeing and none of it meant anything to him. He could be looking at a picture of a Martian landscape for all he knew.

"Yeah." Natalya nodded, her lips moving as if she were counting. "She's fine. Now, anyway."

"And was she not fine before?" Zane asked. Natalya's narrowed eye focus on the screen was making him uneasy. He'd seen her scan people more than once, and she didn't usually pay much attention, just storing the records for cross-referencing later. Of course this scan was different, since she was looking for injuries, but if she wasn't finding anything, why was she watching so closely?

Not bothering to answer, Natalya typed a few quick keystrokes, and suddenly the screen became recognizably the bones of a hand. "Look at that." Natalya almost sighed. "What could she have done?"

"Um, no idea?" Zane said, a hint of impatience entering his voice. "What are we looking at?"

"Oh, right." She glanced at him as if she'd forgotten he was there, and almost reluctantly touched several spots on the screen. "See those light spots? That's calcification. She's broken the bones there. Five places, I think, and probably all around the same time, so somehow she really smashed up her hand. But that break pattern—I don't know how she could have done that." She stared at her own hand speculatively, as if trying to imagine a way to break the bones in those locations.

"But she's okay now?" Zane asked, and this time the impatience was real. Was there a problem or not?

"Um, yeah." Natalya glanced at him again before shifting in her chair, and then typing a few more words so that the screen shifted back to meaningless gray blobs.

"Nat?"

She sighed, and typed again, this time for several sentences. The screen turned into a picture of a skeleton. "Count the light spots."

Zane glanced. There were a lot of light spots. "What are they?"

"Places where bones have been broken in the past. Both bones of her right arm in multiple places, her collarbone, the ribs at least a few times, and her jaw, ouch. Plus the hand. And maybe a bone in the foot. Most of them happened a long time ago, but it wasn't one bad accident. You can tell from the levels of calcification that they occurred at different times. The hand was recent." She looked at Zane thoughtfully. "Your girl has lived a dangerous life."

"My girl?" Zane's surprise showed. "She's not mine. This is only the second time I've met her." He didn't mention the number of times he'd thought of her in the month since her interview. It was more than a few.

"Oh, right." Natalya busied herself with the keyboard again, looking embarrassed.

"Okay, sister mine, what do you know that I don't?"

She grinned at him. "Well, there's that entire medical school curriculum, for one thing."

"You know that's not what I meant. You saw something, didn't you?"

"And you know I prefer not to talk about those things. The future is ours to control. Anything I see is just a possibility."

Zane sighed. His sister had inherited his father's gift—the only one in the family to do so. Max might call himself a serendipidist, but the rest of the world would have called him a precognitive psychic. Not always, not consistently, and not always accurately, but sometimes, and often when it counted, he could see the future.

So could Nat. But unlike their father, she tried not to act on her knowledge and not to share it. Her exceptions were random—Akira's two-year contract had to have been one of them, Zane suspected—but rare. And once she decided not to talk, nothing short of an act of God would get her mouth open. Zane wasn't even going to try.

"So how do you think she broke all those bones?" he asked, nodding toward Akira.

Natalya glanced in that direction and frowned. "You could ask her. But . . ."

Zane raised his eyebrows when she didn't continue. "Go on."

She was quiet again.

"Come on, Nat. Tell me what you know." This was right in front of him, if he only knew how to read the scans.

"This might fall under doctor-patient confidentiality," she finally said.

"I'm in the room with you, watching the scans, and she knows I'm here. She could have gone to a perfectly nice hospital, and she didn't, so tell me what you see." He didn't often dig his heels in, but he felt almost annoyed that Nat knew more about Akira than he did. Bad enough that she wouldn't tell him what her gift revealed, but he knew he ought to be able to figure this out for himself.

"Ribs, jaw, spiral fractures on the arms? And that hand . . ." Nat pulled up the image of the skeletal hand again, and looked at it, shaking her head.

"What about them?" he asked. He glanced back through the window. Nat's typing had caused the table to slide out of the machine, and Akira was sitting up.

"If this was an emergency room, and she was here with fresh injuries, I'd be sending in a social worker before I let her leave. And probably a police officer, too," Nat said, before adding with a sigh, "But since all I've got is you, go bandage her abrasions."

≈CHAPTER FIVE≈

Akira waited restlessly. The metal table, the dim light, the feel of the cotton hospital gown against her skin—all were bringing back memories, and while she was trying to feel grateful for Zane's concern and Natalya's helpfulness, mostly she just wanted out. Quickly.

The door to the room opened and Zane entered, trying to balance a few boxes with one hand while pushing the door with the other, not looking at her. He was unsmiling, Akira noticed, his brows drawn down over his blue-gray eyes, his face somber.

She frowned. She felt all right—bruised and stinging, but not seriously hurt. "I'm okay, aren't I?"

His brows went up, almost startled. "Oh, yeah, you're fine." He smiled, but Akira could tell that it was slightly forced. "Nat has delegated me to bandage your scrapes," he adding, holding up his supplies.

She looked down at the abrasions, turning her arms out to show them to him. They were just brush burns, really, not deep or bleeding, but the skin was raw and red. "I hope you have some big Band-Aids."

He grimaced sympathetically. "Nat gave me gauze and tape. GD's not a hospital, but we do a fair amount of medical research here so we're well stocked. Nat could probably handle anything short of the zombie apocalypse." He dropped the boxes on the table, opened them and took out what he needed, then moved to stand in front of her.

As he took her right arm in his warm hands, Akira closed her eyes and clenched her teeth. This was not going to feel good. She couldn't prevent a wince at his touch, but pressed her lips together and stayed silent while Zane cleaned the abrasions and applied an antibiotic ointment lightly, first on one arm, and then the next.

"All done," he said. Akira took a deep breath. The antibiotic must have had a numbing cream in it, because the stinging pain was starting to fade.

"Pretty stoic, aren't you?" Zane asked, handing her the tape to hold. Akira shrugged. What was there to say to that? They were just scrapes, after all. He unfolded the gauze and began positioning it on her arm, a slight awkwardness revealing his unfamiliarity with the job.

"So, are you an extreme sports fan?" His question almost sounded casual, but Akira looked at his bent head warily. Extreme sports?

"No. Why do you ask?" she replied.

"My sister tells me you've broken quite a few bones in your time."

Akira glanced at the window that opened onto the room with the computer screens. Hmm, she supposed the scan could have shown that, couldn't it? "I guess I've broken my share."

He reached for the tape, and she gave it back to him. Casually, he ripped a piece off with his teeth, before asking, "But not skateboarding? Or maybe some mountain climbing? Skydiving?"

"No." Did she look like a skateboarder? She smiled a little at the idea, trying to picture herself flying off a ramp and spinning in the air.

Finished with her first arm, he looked up, catching her gaze and holding it, his eyes intent. "Is there someone I can kill for you?" he asked.

Startled, she lost her smile. "Excuse me?" He'd said those words with such seriousness.

"Is the person who beat you still alive?" he asked the question patiently, without anger, not looking away.

She bit her lip. And then she pulled her eyes away from his, almost by force of will, looking to the side to get away from his focused stare without dropping her gaze. "It's not that simple." But then she realized that the easiest answer was also at least mostly true. "No."

"Good." He nodded, then patted her arm gently, setting it down and reaching for the other one.

She felt a rush of warmth for him. His question was possibly the sweetest thing anyone had ever said to her. Sort of. It was also just the tiniest bit scary. Zane didn't look like a killer, but did she know what a killer would look like? "What would you have done if I'd said yes?"

"Called my brother," he answered, looking up at her with a wry grin. "I admit, it's not my area of expertise, but if you were in danger, Lucas would take care of it." He finished the sentence sounding grim, before turning back to the gauze and tape.

"I'm not. But . . . thank you. I think."

"He does draw the line at murder, though," Zane continued more cheerfully. "Knowing Lucas, he'd come up with some complicated plan that would require middle of the night road trips, secret rendezvous, untraceable cell phones, and way too much thinking. But at the end of the day, you'd be as safe as the universe would allow."

"Does he work for General Directions, too?" she asked. Did he have something to do with why that security guard looked so over-qualified to be sitting in an office building on a weekend? What did this company do exactly, anyway?

"Yep. He's on the road most of the time, though. He does a lot of our government work." Zane finished smoothing down the tape on her second arm, just as the door opened and Natalya entered, carrying a prescription pad.

Smiling, but with a mild note of reproach in her voice, she said, "You could have let her get dressed first, Zane."

Zane looked momentarily surprised and then, as if for the first time, seemed to notice what Akira was wearing. Her hospital gown was the typical loose-fitting, light-weight cotton, white with a pattern of tiny flowers, but a cool breeze where the ties gaped in the back, revealing her bare skin. Natalya had told her to take everything off, and she'd thought nothing of it, but under Zane's gaze, she suddenly felt very aware of her lack of underwear.

"I'm sorry, I was thinking more about what was under—I mean, I was thinking about the scan—" he stuttered to a halt, taking a hasty step backwards. "I'll just . . . I'll wait outside." He gestured to the door, and then made a quick exit, dropping the tape on the table.

"I think I embarrassed him." Natalya sounded surprised, looking after him. She turned back to Akira, who could feel her cheeks turning pink with heat as a flush of warmth raced through her. "And I embarrassed you, too," she said. "I'm sorry."

Akira shook her head, trying not to blush even harder. "It's fine, really."

"He doesn't embarrass easily," Natalya added, looking at Akira with a slight frown.

Akira shifted, feeling acutely self-conscious.

"Well, let me just take a look." Natalya checked the gauze on Akira's arms, and gave her some quick instructions for care, ignoring

Akira's uneasiness. She handed Akira a paper prescription for painkillers and added, "We're a research facility, not a traditional office, so I can't call it in for you. You'll have to stop by a pharmacy."

Akira took the paper dutifully, nodding, but the thought of finding a pharmacy seemed almost overwhelming. She was going to have to call a mechanic to get the Taurus fixed. And a rental car agency to get another car for the time being. Or maybe a taxi service? For just a moment, she yearned to be back in California, back in her familiar world.

"I'll let you get dressed now." Natalya seemed to be looking right through Akira. "And don't worry, everything's going to be fine."

Easy for her to say, Akira thought as she returned to the small room she'd started in, and quickly scrambled back into her clothes, pulling her shirt over her head with a wince of pain. She could feel that her hair was a mess, the wispy dark layers tangled, and she hastily finger-combed it, wishing for a mirror.

A tentative knock on the door interrupted her, and Akira pulled it open. Zane was standing on the other side, one hand up to the door, the other holding his cell phone to his ear. "Yes, Dad," he was saying patiently. "Let me just see when will work." He dropped the phone to his side and said, "You want to meet my dad for dinner tonight? We can swing by a drugstore, drop off your prescription, then pick it up when I take you back to your hotel after we eat."

Akira opened her mouth to protest that he didn't need to do all that, and then shut it again. No need to be stupid about this—if he was willing to drive her to the places she needed to go, she should just be grateful. Plus, she was eager to meet the mysterious Dr. Max Latimer. "Sure, that's fine."

He put a hand under her elbow and led her down the hallway and into the elevator, still talking into the cellphone. That moment of awareness spurred by how little she'd been wearing hadn't passed: Akira felt the warmth of his touch as acutely as if it were a deliberate stroke rather than a casual familiarity. Her heart was beating a little too quickly, and there was a low-level tingle teasing her stomach. Oh, dear. There were probably a dozen reasons why it was a bad idea to be feeling attracted to this guy, starting with the fact that she had a two-year contract to work for him.

But he was insanely cute, she admitted to herself. That messy hair, the grin, the casual ease in the way he moved? And then there was the sweet way he'd taken care of her injuries, his careful touch and concern. She wondered what he'd be like in bed, whether he was one of those guys that was all about the final moments or whether he was playful and lingering—and then he snapped his phone shut and said, in a businesslike tone, "I've arranged for Dillon's car to be towed and repaired. We'll need to talk about your lease."

Oh, right. She was here under totally false pretenses. They hadn't hired her for her research skills and scientific knowledge; they'd hired her to talk to spirits. And that was not something she was going to do. The tingle in her stomach didn't exactly die, but she firmly suppressed it as she tugged her elbow free.

"What about my lease?" she asked, as they exited the elevator, and headed out of the building. It had gotten late in the afternoon but the sun was still bright, the sky a clear blue. A tow truck was parked next to the black car, a vaguely familiar dark-haired man in blue jeans and a t-shirt leaning against it, his hands in his pockets.

"Hey, Dave," Zane greeted him, tossing him the car keys.

The man quickly pulled his hands out and snatched the keys out of the air. "You serious about the rush job?"

"Yep." Akira, following a few steps behind Zane, saw that Dillon was seated, cross-legged, on the roof of the car. He waved at her, but didn't say anything. She smiled at him, grateful that he remembered not to talk to her in front of living people.

Dave shook his head. "Kyle says sure thing, then. For triple time, he'd bang more than—" he faltered to a halt, as he noticed Akira, and then continued smoothly, as if he'd never paused, "—he's happy to fix a dent and get some new air bags installed. And you're in luck; he can pull the bags from a loaner he's got. You can get this thing back tomorrow." He gave the car's tire a gentle kick.

"Nice," Zane said approvingly. He pulled open the door of the car and stuck his head in. "Hey, Dillon, Dave's going to take the car, but it's only until tomorrow. You want Kyle to—I don't know, play you music or something?"

He looked over his shoulder at Akira, who was paused by the hood, staring at him. "What's he say?"

"Uh, who ya' talking to, dude?" Dave asked, while Akira compressed her lips together. She couldn't believe Zane. What did he think he was doing?

"Car's haunted," Zane answered, straightening. He gestured

toward Akira with his chin. "She can see ghosts."

Akira's eyes widened and her mouth opened and then she glared. Did the man not have a speck of discretion? At this rate, the entire world was going to know she was crazy.

Dave's brows raised, but he managed not to let go of whatever skeptical comment was on his tongue, taking a few steps forward and holding out his hand to shake hands with Akira. "Dave Voigt," he said. "A pleasure."

"Akira Malone," she sighed, shaking his hand and wishing she dared give a fake name. But Zane would probably give her away immediately if she did.

"So what's he say?" Zane repeated.

"Yeah, what's he say?" Dave grinned at her, and it wasn't quite a smirk.

Damn it, she didn't know what to do. She glanced at Dillon, who shrugged. "Talking Heads?" he offered.

She frowned. It seemed like an odd choice from a teenage boy. She'd thought he was a recent ghost, within a few years, but she supposed his casual attire could have been from any late twentieth century era. Still, if Zane was his uncle, and had known him in life, he couldn't be that old. "Aren't you kind of young for them? They ought to be from before you were even born."

She ignored the surprised look from Dave, standing next to her. Zane, following her gaze, realized that Dillon was outside the car. He stepped back and shut the car door.

"My dad's a big fan," Dillon replied. "I used to listen to them all the time. And Kyle'll have 'em on CD in the garage."

Well, okay, then. "Talking Heads," Akira said.

Zane nodded, and for a moment, Dave looked startled, his eyes widening, body straightening. Then he relaxed and said, "Nice. Your dad must be stoked. Hey, Dillon."

It was Akira's turn to look surprised. What the hell was wrong with people in this town? Did they believe anything they were told?

~CHAPTER SIX~

Akira argued with Zane for ten minutes, then spent the rest of the car ride fuming.

How could he not understand what a terrible idea it was to let people know that she saw ghosts? It was dangerous!

If they didn't believe in ghosts, they'd think she was crazy.

If they did believe in ghosts, it would be even worse. She was a scientist, a rational researcher who believed in the laws of logic and the scientific method. Seeing ghosts was a problem. A disability, even. It wasn't something she wanted people to know about her.

And she'd tried telling him so, but he'd just brushed off her concerns with an airy, "Dave's seen weirder, and Nat is weirder. Don't worry about it."

Weirder! His doctor sister? Natalya had seemed as normal as blueberry pie to Akira. And having her perfectly reasonable anxiety dismissed was infuriating.

Plus, there were the ghosts. Zane didn't understand the risks, and his easy acceptance of his nephew's presence didn't mean that he'd be as ready to believe in the darker side of spirit energy. Hundreds of years of scary stories weren't all wrong: not all ghosts were like Dillon. But how to tell Zane so without sounding insane? Or would that be more insane?

As he pulled the car into a parking space on the town's main street, Zane said cheerfully, "You're a sulker, aren't you?"

A sulker? Akira had never had a sibling, but she recognized the type. He was a button-pusher. "And you're a younger brother, aren't you?"

He laughed as she got out of the car. "I'm serious," she repeated across the roof, as he walked around to the curbside. "This isn't something that I want people to know."

"It's not like I'm putting it on CNN," he said reasonably, as she fell into step beside him. They were headed to the restaurant she'd seen on her first quick visit to the town, the one that looked something like a cross between a café and a diner. "I told my sister, and she was bound to find out anyway because of Dillon. And Dave won't tell anyone."

"Natalya's not—she wasn't—" Akira didn't know how to ask the question politely. She was sure that Natalya wasn't Dillon's mother from her calm reaction to the idea that he was a ghost, but she knew very little about the Latimer family.

For a fleeting second, Zane looked grim. "No. Lucas, the brother I mentioned, is Dillon's father. He's not around much, though. My parents were raising Dillon."

"Losing a child is hard, I know. Is that why your dad—" Akira searched for the words and finally settled on, "—has been looking for a medium?" It seemed more tactful than saying, "lost his mind and decided that ghosts were real?" Sure, she knew ghosts were real, but that's because she could see and hear them. Why would someone who could do neither decide to chase such a pipe dream?

"Dillon and my mom died three days apart," Zane replied. "Dillon of a drug overdose, and my mom from a stroke. A couple of years ago, my dad met the woman who told him that the car was haunted, but she—well, ever since, he's been looking for someone who could communicate with their spirits."

Akira barely heard the words after overdose. Poor Zane. To lose both his mother and his nephew in the same week. She'd only ever had her father, but the emptiness that filled their house in the weeks and months after his death had been horrible. And his death hadn't been unexpected: untimely, yes, but they'd known he'd lost his fight against cancer for weeks before he died. And an overdose? For a teenager as young as Dillon? How truly sad.

"I'm so sorry for your loss," she said.

He looked down at her. In the late afternoon sunlight, his eyes were bluer, almost the color of the sky behind them, and she could see in his expression how hard it had been. And then he grinned at her, and said, "Yeah, it wasn't a great week," as he pushed open the door and gestured for her to precede him inside.

The restaurant was an eclectic mix of styles: as if someone with modern taste had taken over an old-style diner without the money or time to renovate from the ground up. The floor was ugly gray linoleum, and there was a long plain lunch-style counter in the middle of the room, with an open kitchen galley beyond it. But small tables were covered with bright linens, and set with colorful cloth napkins, and a row of private booths along one wall had wooden tabletops and comfy cloth seating.

As Akira looked around, noticing the fanciful artwork on the walls, she realized that the restaurant was crowded, almost every table full, and that most of the people in it seemed to be looking in her direction. Or was it Zane they were looking at? She glanced at him.

"Small town, new face," he murmured in her ear as he put a comforting hand on her back and steered her toward a back corner booth, nodding and greeting people at the tables they passed. "Nothing to worry about."

She wasn't worried, she thought defensively. Or not exactly worried. She just maybe wished she'd found a brush, a mirror, and a little make-up back at General Directions. Facing a roomful of curious strangers looking like you'd recently been in a car accident wasn't a confidence boost.

There was a man seated at the booth Zane was headed to, his back to the restaurant. This must be the eccentric Max Latimer, Akira thought. As she slid into the booth across from him, he looked up from his book and smiled at her, and almost involuntarily, Akira smiled back. Dark hair gone gray at the temples, blue eyes bordered with deeply engraved laugh lines, bushy brows and a smile that lit up his face—she could see his resemblance to his children and grandson.

"You must be the medium," he said, putting out his hand for her to shake.

Akira's smile disappeared immediately. "I am not a medium," she said, turning to Zane with a glare as he seated himself on the bench next to her. What had Zane said to his father? Hadn't she made herself perfectly clear when she told him she could see ghosts? Mediums got messages from invisible spirits. They were spiritualists who believed in some mystical "other side." They held séances and went into trances!

"She sees ghosts," Zane told his father. "Apparently there's a difference."

The sympathy that Akira had felt for him moments earlier evaporated as her annoyance returned. Had he not listened to a word she'd said?

"Aw, come on," he said to her, apparently reading her expression. "We had to tell him."

"No!" she said. "No, we didn't. This is not—I don't—I'm a scientist. A physicist. With, I admit, a slightly unusual—" she paused, searching for the right word.

"Gift?" Max offered.

Akira shook her head, rejecting his choice, and finally settled on one of her own. "Quirk. It's just a quirk. And I don't want people to know about it."

Max and Zane exchanged looks. "Tassamara is a town that attracts people who have quirks," Max said. "No one here will think anything of it."

Akira sighed. It was a weird little town, she had to acknowledge that. But that didn't mean that seeing ghosts was a socially acceptable skill to have. "I don't like ghosts," she said slowly, trying to find the right words to explain how she felt, but before she could continue, Max interrupted her.

"Miss Malone," he started, and then smiled and reached across the table, patting the back of her hand comfortingly. "Akira. You leased a car with a ghost in it. You rented a house that's known to be haunted. You can't be that afraid of your association with the spirit world."

The spirit world? Oh, hell, Akira thought, as she protested, "Every place the realtor showed me was haunted!"

"The last thing on the list was a nice little modern apartment," Zane said mildly. "Fifteen miles outside of town, so not exactly convenient, but brand-new and unlikely to have any spectral tenants."

"You knew the properties she was going to show me?" Akira asked.

He shrugged. "Perception tests, remember. We didn't find you because we were looking for a physicist."

"But I am a physicist," Akira protested. "Look, seeing ghosts—it's just some kind of energy. That's all. It's not entirely crazy to think that human beings might be more than matter or chemicals. We're complex systems. Yes, I've got this ability, but it's like being a super-taster or a tetrachromat, just some genetic variation in a sensory faculty. Rare, obviously, but then so are tetrachromats."

"Super-taster I know," Max said. "Picky eaters, but with more taste buds than most people have, so food tastes more intense to them. But what's a tetrachromat?"

"Most people have three types of cones in our eyes, each of which responds to a different wavelength of visible lengths. Three cones, so we're trichromats," Akira explained. "But some people—women, most likely, because of the two X chromosomes—could have four types of cones. Theoretically, they could see into the ultraviolet, like zebra fish can. An average human being can distinguish about a million shades of color, but a tetrachromat could distinguish about a hundred million shades."

Momentarily distracted by the idea, she added thoughtfully, "It'd be hell to get dressed; nothing would ever look like it matched." Then she shook her head and continued, "It is scientifically possible that I have a sense that allows me to see energy. A type of energy. A type of energy that other people can't perceive, like seeing into the ultraviolet, only not exactly like that because. . ." She let her words trail off as she saw that Max was smiling gently at her.

"You hear them too, don't you?" Zane asked. "How does that work if it's a visual sense?"

He was so damn matter-of-fact, thought Akira. There was something profoundly annoying about it. She sighed. "Okay, so it's a little more than a visual sense. Seeing different wavelengths, plus hearing different frequencies. Or maybe my brain just translates the extra sense into something more comprehensible to me? The point is, it's not who I am. It's like being left-handed, or having perfect pitch—just a, a quirk." She waved a hand dismissively.

"A quirk that allows you to speak to my grandson," Max said. "And, I hope, to my wife."

Akira wanted to cry. Relatives. Oh, how she hated dealing with the relatives. "Yes," she said simply, and then shrugged. "Or maybe, I don't know about your wife. But yes, I can talk to Dillon. And?"

"What do you mean?" Max asked.

"What then?" Akira asked in return. "Yes, I can talk to your relatives. So can you, for that matter, but okay, I can maybe actually have a conversation with them. And then what?"

"Can't you help them? Help them move on or do whatever it is they're supposed to be doing?"

She shook her head. "No. Ghosts—they just are. They're not a problem to be solved. Well, except sometimes for me. But they're not a thing that needs fixing, any more than, well, than say, lightning needs fixing. They're just energy. Leftover energy. "

Max rubbed his chin. "But why are they still here?"

Akira exhaled, a quick breath that was almost a laugh. "Ask me about low-temperature collision dynamics. You'd get a better answer."

"I'm not actually interested in low-temperature collision dynamics," Max responded, voice dry.

Akira's mouth twisted. It wasn't a smile. "Nor sonoluminescence, I assume?"

"I don't even know what that is," Max admitted.

Akira closed her eyes and sighed, inwardly cursing herself. She should have asked more questions. She should have remembered that things that look too good to be true are too good to be true. "I don't know why ghosts exist," she said. "For obvious reasons, it's not a subject that's easily researched. But I don't fix them, I don't make them go away, and—before you ask—I don't know anything about any white lights."

She pressed her lips together. Across the table, Max was silent, his disappointment obvious. "I should go back to California," Akira realized. "If I had known you were—" She let the sentence end there. She didn't want to accuse either of them. And yet her disappointment was acute. She had wanted to believe that this would be a place for her, that she had found a new home.

"Not a chance," said Zane.

She glanced at him. Sure, she'd signed a contract, but there was nothing in it about ghosts.

"I bought you a very nice digital oscilloscope, and I took the money for it out of Smithson's budget," Zane continued. "If you don't show up tomorrow and play with it, he'll get annoyed, and that's never fun. Grace will yell at me—it'll be a whole messy thing." He grinned at her and it was such a comforting smile that it almost felt like he'd rubbed a consoling hand along her back.

"Yes," agreed Max. He too smiled at her, and if his smile was a little more strained, a little more disappointed, it was still a smile. "Regardless of whether you can help me, this is a good place for you. And I'm sure your research will prove interesting." For a moment, his eyes stilled, and then he added in a tone of mild delight, "Hmm, and profitable, too. That's nice."

"Profitable?" Akira was startled.

"Not that sono-thing, though, I don't think. Something else."

Akira looked back at Zane. What was his father talking about?

"Max is psychic," Zane said. "He can see the future."

Psychic.

Right.

Were they kidding?

A small smile was playing around Zane's lips, but he wasn't looking at her. He seemed focused on catching the attention of their waitress.

According to Einstein, past, present, and future were simply a stubbornly persistent illusion. Akira wasn't a quantum physicist herself, but she knew that they postulated that on an atomic level, the future could be known. If they were right, then theoretically seeing the future could be possible. But still, it sounded highly unlikely to her. Although not really any more unlikely than seeing ghosts.

Maybe it was time for some basic scientific inquiry. "So, did you know we'd be having this conversation?" She tried not to let any emotion slip into the words, to make them as calm and neutral as she could, but even she could hear the hint of skepticism that slipped out.

Max's smile was approving. "No. No, if I could see everything, I'm sure I'd be institutionalized. It would be impossible to function. No, I just sometimes know the outcome of an event before it happens. Rather random events, it seems. There are events I would have given a great deal to have foreseen that were obscured to me." The sadness in his eyes didn't match his smile.

"He's mostly good with money," Zane said, turning his attention back to the table.

"Money?" Akira was startled. That seemed so practical.

"Things that make money, really," Max corrected his son. "The money itself was your mother."

Akira raised her eyebrows at Max, encouraging him to go on, and he continued. "My wife was the driving force behind General Directions. The company is primarily a holding company. We buy and sell shares of other companies, and sometimes pick up useful patents. As I'm sure you can imagine, foreknowledge is an asset when it comes to dabbling in investments."

"Shouldn't that be illegal?" Akira was fascinated. It had never occurred to her to look for such a pragmatic use for her own quirk. Not that ghosts were likely to be useful when it came to buying stocks, but they could have been helpful in other ways, she supposed. Maybe?

"Oh, probably," Max agreed. "But I wouldn't want to be the politician trying to get the law passed."

"Or the lawyer trying to prosecute," Zane said. "It's tough to prove. Turns out that knowing the future looks a lot like insider trading from the outside, at least to the SEC, so we've had some experience."

Max waved his hand, as if brushing away the SEC. "We've worked all that out."

Akira was still trying to put the pieces together. "If it's a holding company, why do you have research labs?" she asked. The labs she'd seen on her first tour were impressively well-stocked and the scanner that Nat had used earlier in the day had to be a multi-million dollar piece of equipment. That didn't fit the picture of a company that only invested in other companies.

"I like research," Max answered, as if that was all that needed to be said.

"Got to spend the money on something," Zane murmured to Akira. "Mom always spent it on making more of it, but Dad uses part of the profits for his interests."

"We've got some fascinating projects underway. Some, of course, explore our, well, quirks, if you will, but we've funded some biochemical research that's quite amazing. And there's a quantum teleportation project that you might be interested in." Max sounded eager to share, and Akira heard the words with a surge of curiosity. Quirks?

"You're researching psychic phenomena?" she asked, not sure how she felt about that. Academically, of course, it was disastrous. Her one speculative paragraph had led to stern words from her department head, whispers in the staff room, mocking jokes from her colleagues, and a seeming end to her academic career.

"I hire people with gifts," Max said. "Or interesting ideas. And then see what they do. Often that means researching the phenomena that affect them directly."

Akira didn't really know much about business, having spent her life in academia, but Max's tactics sounded risky to her. Maybe he really could see the future: the company might need the advantage just to survive.

"Ah, finally," Zane said, as a waitress approached, balancing three plates of food.

"Here you go." The teenage waitress had short blonde curls and way too much eye make-up, but she smiled brightly as she placed the plates on the table, one in front of each of them. Akira's held a cheeseburger, thick and juicy, the lettuce green, the tomato lushly red, and fries that were still sizzling. But she hadn't ordered a cheeseburger. In fact, she hadn't ordered anything.

"What is this?" Zane was looking at his plate with an expression of mild dismay.

"I dunno. I've never seen it before." The waitress glanced over her shoulder at the open kitchen and dropped her voice to a whisper. "Do you want me to take it back? Maggie'll be madder 'n heck."

"I think maybe you got the plates wrong," Max said to the waitress, not unkindly, as he picked up his fork. His plate held grilled salmon and broccoli, Akira noted.

"Do you want this?" Zane asked Akira, his doubt obvious.

Akira looked at Zane's food: golden rice sprinkled with chunks of cauliflower, carrots, green beans, and potatoes, almonds and raisins. "It's vegetable biryani," she said with relief. "And yes, I want it." As she passed her plate over to Zane and he slid his rice dish along the table to her, she asked Max, "How did you know that?"

"Know what?" he asked, taking a bite of salmon.

"Know what I'd want to eat." Akira was pragmatic about food: she ate what was put in front of her. But when she cooked for herself, she mostly ate vegetarian. Had Max had her investigated? Or was this his foresight in action?

"Oh, I didn't," he replied, as she began to eat. "I ordered three specials when I came in. Maggie decides what they'll be."

"Maggie?"

"It's her place," Max replied. "She took it over six, maybe seven years ago. Used to be a diner—your basic fried eggs and bacon for breakfast, meatloaf and potatoes for dinner. Not a bad place but nothing special. Maggie shook it up a bit."

The biryani was terrific, the rice soft, the spice with the perfect level of kick. Akira ate it thoughtfully. Vegetable biryani, in the middle of nowhere, Florida. For that matter, vegetarian food, in the middle of nowhere, Florida. And Max was psychic. And Tassamara was a town of psychics.

"No menus?" she finally asked.

"For visitors, yeah," Zane answered.

She nodded, taking that in. She was beginning to understand what other people must feel like when she told them she could see ghosts. There was doubt, and then a cautious interest, and then total confusion.

"So the town. . ."

"Attracts people with gifts, yes." Max nodded. "We look for them, too, and find them and bring them here, but some show up on their own."

Akira looked around the restaurant. She wondered how many of the people in it were like her. Not that they could see ghosts, of course: Max wouldn't have been looking for a medium for so long if mediums were easily found. But keepers of secrets that most of the world scoffed at?

"Vampires? Werewolves? Ectoplasmic blobs?" she finally asked.

Max looked mystified by the question, but Zane grinned. "No, no, and you'd probably know better on the last. Although I should probably say, not to the best of our knowledge. We've never met any."

Akira ate another bite of rice. Could this be an elaborate practical joke? "You realize this is a little tough to believe."

"Zane's best at providing proof," Max replied readily.

Akira glanced at Zane. He was psychic, too? That was unexpected. "Can you tell me—um—what I'm going to eat for breakfast tomorrow morning?"

"Yogurt," he replied without hesitation and then chuckled at the look on her face. "Did I get it right?"

"Yes," she replied, but something about the laugh in his eyes was making her feel more defensive than convinced.

Max shook his head. "You give psychics a bad name, Zane." He sighed. "That was a cold read. Don't listen to him. He doesn't know anything about the future."

"Rabbit food, California girl, easy guess," Zane agreed. He was watching Akira and she shifted under his gaze. His laugh, the warmth in his look—that tingle was back and more inappropriate than ever. But she could feel her heart picking up its pace a little, her pulse accelerating.

"A cold read?" Akira asked, pulling her eyes away from Zane with an effort, and looking at Max.

"There are a lot more fake psychics in the world than real ones. A cold read is when a pretender makes likely guesses and uses your responses to improve further guesses. Zane's got a gift but it's not precognition."

"I find things," Zane told her. "Lost anything recently?"

"No." Akira thought for a moment. "But most of my belongings are on a truck somewhere. Can you tell me where it is?"

He nodded, and held out his hand to her, palm up. She looked at it and raised her eyebrows questioningly. "It's easier if I'm touching you," he explained.

Touching her? That seemed like a bad idea. But Akira placed her hand on his, and as his warm fingers closed around hers, she tried hard to ignore the melting feeling that was starting in her belly. His eyes were closed and she watched him in fascination, wondering what he felt, what was happening inside his head.

And then his eyelids flickered open and his eyes caught hers, the pupils dark and dilated in the gray-blue, and for just a moment he was leaning toward her—and then, hastily, he dropped her hand and pulled back and said, with a slight rasp to his voice, "Outside Jacksonville. The truck will get here tomorrow."

Tomorrow? It could be a guess. But she'd find out soon.

❧CHAPTER SEVEN☙

Akira paced across the porch.

If only she'd gotten here before the movers. But they'd arrived too early. She had only the loosest grasp on Florida geography, but Zane could have been right the evening before, when he'd said her belongings were outside Jacksonville. Either way, the moving company had made good time. She'd gotten the call at the hotel and by the time she arranged for a ride to the house, they were here. Unfortunately, that meant she'd had no chance to introduce herself to the ghosts.

She'd been anxious enough about those introductions. It had seemed so simple when she'd made the decision to rent the house. The turret room, the lovely backyard, Rose's enthusiasm, Dillon . . . it all added up to a worthwhile risk. But she'd imagined herself starting by calmly sitting down in the kitchen, talking to the ghostly inhabitants, setting some ground rules, establishing a few guidelines for how they could all live together. If the ghosts were typical, they'd have questions for her—questions that she probably couldn't answer—and maybe a few tasks that they hoped she'd do. As long as no relatives were involved, she didn't mind running a few ghostly errands.

Instead, she was forced to try to pretend she couldn't hear Rose's running commentary as the movers carried her belongings into the house.

"Yes, that goes into this front room." Akira directed the movers carrying her sofa up the front steps.

"Ooh, those muscles are dreamy." Rose jumped onto the piece of moving furniture and draped herself over it, eying the young man in a tight t-shirt who was carrying the front end. "You're just my type. I wonder if you like to dance. I'd love to go dancing with you." As the movers placed the sofa, Rose slid up the seat to the end, until the man lifting it gave a convulsive shiver.

"Cold in here," he said to the other mover.

Akira chewed on her lower lip, as Rose sighed, and collapsed back onto the sofa melodramatically, before springing to her feet again and following the movers back outside.

"Now that's a pretty chair," Rose said about a floral-patterned wing-back chair the mover was pulling out of the truck. "Awfully old-fashioned, though. I guess you inherited all your furniture. You don't look like the flowery type, bless your heart. I mean, those clothes. And that lipstick. No, I'm thinking that was your grandma's chair."

With an effort, Akira kept from looking down at her clothes. Jeans and a t-shirt seemed like a practical choice to her. And what was wrong with her lipstick?

"Ooh and speaking of dreamy." Rose clasped both hands together under her chin, and took a deep appreciative breath. Akira followed her gaze and tried not to smile. The black Taurus was parked behind the moving van and Zane was stepping out. Dreamy, huh?

"He can visit us any day," Rose continued. "Look at that hair. I just want to run my fingers through it." It was nice hair, Akira agreed inwardly—dark and wavy, with coppery glints in the sunlight.

After exchanging a few words with the movers who were offloading boxes, Zane headed up the walkway. Spotting Akira on the porch, he grinned at her.

Dropping her hands, Rose clutched the porch post. "Oh, and that smile," she squealed. Akira couldn't resist finally letting her own smile break free. Back at the Taurus, Dillon hovered uncertainly next to the car door, looking up at her. She nodded and tilted her head, a slight gesture to tell him to come on in.

"Jacksonville yesterday evening," Zane drawled as he approached. "You convinced?"

"Not exactly," she answered, stuffing her hands into the front pockets of her jeans and shrugging her shoulders. "Could have been a lucky guess."

"Huh. A skeptic. Not what I would have expected."

"Why? Just because—" Akira stumbled to a halt as the movers walked toward them.

"Television in the living room, ma'am?" one of them asked her.

"No, no," she said hastily. "Put that upstairs, in the bedroom right off the top of the steps. Oh, and hey, bring that flowered chair up there, too, please."

"Oh, yay, a television in my bedroom! And the chair? But that's—the bedroom? My bedroom?" Rose was staring at Akira, and Akira couldn't resist widening her eyes at her.

"Can you see me?" Rose's voice dropped to a whisper. "Can you hear me?"

Akira looked at Dillon, and raised her eyebrows, trying to signal to him to explain to Rose, but he was staring at Rose, mouth agape. Akira looked back at Rose. Oh. Oops.

"How old was Dillon?" she asked Zane.

"When he—?" Zane started and then answered, "Fifteen. Why?"

Lovely. She'd just thrown a fifteen-year-old boy ghost who'd been alone for years into close proximity with an extremely pretty girl ghost. What a good idea that was. She put her hand up to cover her mouth, and the smile that she couldn't contain, and shook her head. Zane was looking at her, waiting for a response. Rose was staring at her. Dillon was staring at Rose. And the movers were still moving boxes and furniture into the house.

"Maybe we should all—I mean, maybe we should go into the kitchen?" she said to Zane. "I could maybe make you some tea?"

"Tea?" His tone didn't conceal his dismay at the idea. "Coffee?" he suggested.

"Green tea is extremely good for you. Polyphenols, antioxidants, lowers your cholesterol—and for a guy whose favorite meal is a cheeseburger and fries, that's probably a good idea."

"It also tastes disgusting. Like drinking grass, and not the entertaining kind."

She rolled her eyes. "I'll make you some nice mint tea, then. It'll taste like gum."

"Can you see me?" Rose repeated urgently, ignoring the conversation that Zane and Akira were having.

"Um, she can, yes," Dillon answered, finally finding his voice, while Akira turned and entered the house, Zane and the ghosts falling into step behind her.

She shivered in the hallway when Rose burst through her, calling for Henry. As they stepped into the kitchen, the older ghost was tucking his newspaper under his arm, saying calmly, "Rose, now, honey, slow down, you're talking so fast I can't understand a word."

"She can see me, Henry, she can see me," Rose burbled. "And look, she brought one of us with her." She gestured, wide-armed, at

Dillon.

"Well, how do you do, son?" Henry reached out to Dillon but his hand passed straight through Dillon's. "Oh." He looked surprised, but Dillon was unconcerned, just turning the shake into a casual wave. He'd gotten over his stunned amazement, Akira noticed, and was now bouncing on his toes with excitement.

Akira looked around the kitchen, debating her next move. With the movers in the house and Zane in the room, she shouldn't talk to the ghosts. Or maybe she should. Maybe it was time to see if Zane was really as nonchalant about the idea as he acted. Then she imagined trying to open her mouth and say hello to the ghosts with him watching, and her heart quailed. She bit her lip uncertainly.

"Aha, a perfect test," Zane said. He was looking around the kitchen, oblivious to the ghostly conversation. The movers had stacked half a dozen boxes on the floor next to the sink, and Zane crossed to them, walking through Henry without blinking, although Akira winced. Running his hand down the sides of the plain brown boxes, he stopped, crouching, at the bottom. "Always the last one."

Standing, he shifted the boxes, and then pulled out the one he'd picked. He looked over his shoulder at Akira, and tilted the box, so that she could see the label on top. In her own careful handwriting, it read "Kitchen, Open First."

"Convinced?" Zane said.

She smiled at him and her moment of uncertainty passed. "You said it yourself; the one you want is always on the bottom."

He was picking at the tape at the edge of the box, pulling it loose. "And I suppose everyone knows that the first thing you need when you've just moved is a way to make hot water taste like dirt?" He grinned up at her, as he pulled the long strip of tape off. "If I was the one who'd packed, this box would hold a bottle opener, a six pack of beer, and a way to play music."

He tucked back the cardboard flaps. On the top of the box lay her iPod speakers, carefully enclosed in bubble wrap.

"Half-right," Akira said. She took out the speakers and handed them to Zane, and then rummaged in the box for her tea kettle, mugs, and the boxes of tea.

"Music?" asked Rose, peering over Zane's shoulder. "Does that play music?"

"It does," Akira answered her, not bothering to explain the part about connecting an iPod to it.

Zane, unwrapping the speakers, glanced at her. Akira took a deep breath. Was she really going to do this? In front of a stranger?

An almost stranger, she corrected herself. An almost stranger who claimed to be psychic. An almost stranger who . . . she paused in her thoughts, before she could go any farther. She wasn't ready to think about him in detail. Not now, not yet. The warm glow when she looked at him was enough of an answer to her always question, was it safe? Yes. Yes, it was safe.

At least she hoped it was.

"I'm Akira," she said to Rose and Henry. "And yes, I can see and hear you."

"But you're living," Rose protested.

"My heavens," said Henry, rocking back a little and looking startled. "I don't know as we've ever met a real medium before."

Akira sighed. Really? Did she have to keep having this conversation? "I'm not a medium."

"She just talks to ghosts," Dillon contributed helpfully. "Not all dead people."

Zane had paused in his unwrapping, and was holding a speaker in one hand, bubble wrap in the other. She could see him trying to follow her gaze, but not seeing anyone.

"Thank you, Dillon." Akira's tone was dry. She supposed she should appreciate his clarification.

"Now, that's real interesting." Henry seemed mildly pleased, but Rose was looking dismayed.

Folding her arms across her chest, she stuck her chin in the air. "Well, I'm not going."

Akira eyed her warily. She didn't like it when ghosts got emotional. "Going where?"

"Aren't you going to try to exorcise us?" Rose dropped her arms, defiance melting away, and Akira relaxed.

"Uh, no, I wasn't planning on it," she answered. "I wouldn't know how. Besides, I thought Dillon might like the company."

"Company!" Rose clapped her hands. "We have company, Henry."

☙❧

Zane watched Akira talking to empty space, and wondered what it was like for her. What did they look like, the ghosts? Were they translucent white shapes? Were they shadows? She'd talked about them being energy: did they look like beings made of energy or did they look human?

Did they look dead? Ugh, that was a creepy thought.

He'd seen Dillon at the hospital. He'd looked gray and cold, the color drained from his lips and skin. Did he look like that now? If he did, Zane was just as glad he couldn't see him. It was strange enough to think that he was in the room, but that time hadn't changed him, that he'd stayed frozen at the moment of his death.

Zane could barely remember what Dillon was like when he died. When he thought about him, he remembered all the stages: the baby Dillon, wide-eyed and peaceful; the toddler Dillon, finally getting real hair after months of wispy feathery strands; the six-year-old Dillon, driving cars up and down the dirt in the garden for endless hours; the nine-year-old Dillon, pontificating about the perfect strategy in some complicated card game. All those Dillons, all those many Dillons, had already been gone the night the fifteen year-old tried to jump start a psychic gift with an overdose of supposedly hallucinogenic drugs.

The idiot.

He returned to unwrapping the speakers, still listening to Akira's one-sided conversation, but trying not to react. He'd seen her wary glance at him. He knew she was uneasy, and he could guess that trust wasn't something she gave lightly. He wanted to be careful.

From their conversation in the car yesterday—maybe it could even be called an argument—he knew that keeping her ability secret was important to her. He didn't really understand why. His mom had always insisted that they keep their gifts private, but she saw them as a competitive business advantage, more akin to the formula for Coca-Cola than skeletons in the closet. It wasn't danger that she worried about. But Akira had made it clear that she thought letting people know she could see ghosts was dangerous.

Maybe she was right. Damn, but he wanted to know about those broken bones. Still, from the way she'd responded yesterday, he wasn't going to get answers any time soon.

And he wasn't going to push. He'd never met anyone who'd been abused before, not that he knew of. Of course, he didn't know for sure that he had now, not really. Still, he knew that he didn't want to do anything that would hurt her. Not now, not ever.

And that meant not showing how absolutely, truly strange it was to be standing here listening to her converse with invisible people.

The doorbell rang, and he put down the speakers. "Want me to get that?"

But Meredith wasn't waiting for a reply. "Hello?" she called out from the front door. "You here, Akira?"

"In the kitchen," Zane answered.

Akira looked anxious, her dark eyes worried. "I didn't have time to talk about this," she said, hurriedly. "But please don't—" and then, as Meredith walked into the kitchen carrying a tin-foil wrapped tray, she fell silent.

Please don't? Hmm, what did she not want him to do?

"Akira, hello, good to see your movers found the place. And Zane, hi, haven't seen you in ages." The currently red-headed real estate agent greeted them cheerfully.

"Hey, Mer." Zane stepped forward and dropped a kiss on her upturned cheek. "How's your mom?"

"Oh, good days and bad, you know how it goes," Meredith replied. "Your dad dropped by for a visit last week, filled her in on all the latest gossip. Did you hear that the youngest Terrell kid got into Yale?"

"Yep." Zane waited for it.

"She's the only one in that family with the brains God gave a squirrel." Meredith sniffed. Zane rubbed his chin to hide his smile. Meredith always had been one to hold a grudge.

But then Meredith frowned. "But what are you doing here, Zane?" she asked. She looked from him to Akira and back again, and Zane could see the moment that she realized that Akira wasn't just a scientist. "Does Akira work for you?" she asked, with a hint of smugness in her smile as if she'd known all along.

Oops.

Lying would be useless: gossip traveled in Tassamara at slightly faster than light speed and if Smithson hadn't already been complaining to anyone who would listen that Zane was usurping his prerogatives, Zane didn't know the man. So Zane shrugged, and said, "Yep."

Meredith paused, as if waiting for more, but when he didn't say anything else and Akira just looked puzzled, she quirked an eyebrow, and then continued smoothly, "Well, I just dropped by to bring you this, Akira. A little housewarming present, compliments of Maggie down at the bistro. She said to tell you she's real glad you've moved to town."

"Thank you." Akira took the tray that Meredith handed her uncertainly. Zane wondered what was in it. Maggie liked cooking weird food; she must be happy to have found an appreciative audience.

"Apparently you're more interesting than the rest of us," Meredith said with a laugh.

"I haven't met Maggie yet?" Akira's words were half-question, half-statement, and she glanced at Zane. He could see that she was wondering why Maggie would take an interest in her and he smiled to reassure her. Maggie didn't like being interrupted while she was cooking or they would have introduced her last night. But meeting Maggie was almost beside the point: if you walked in the door of the bistro, she knew what you wanted to eat.

"No?" Meredith raised one shoulder. "That never troubles Maggie. Although if you liked the same food as this one here," she said, gesturing to Zane, "she probably wouldn't be bothering to cook for you."

"Hey, nothing wrong with burgers and fries," Zane protested mildly. "And I like Maggie's meatloaf."

Meredith rolled her eyes. "Maggie told me what it was, but I can't say as I recall exactly. Aloo-something."

Akira peeked under the tinfoil. "Aloo gobi. Yum."

It didn't sound yum. It sounded spicy.

"Well, you enjoy. Let me know if you need anything, Akira, and I'll see both of you later." In a typical whirl, Meredith was gone.

"What did that mean?" Akira asked him immediately, setting the dish down on the kitchen counter.

"What?" he asked, cursing silently. "That Maggie likes to cook weird stuff? What's in that?" He poked at the dish.

"No, that I work for you."

Oh, man. She was going to be pissed, he just knew it. He needed to think of a way to phrase his explanation carefully.

"Special affairs? What does that mean?" she continued.

But he hadn't said anything. He frowned.

"I—what?" Akira grabbed at her hair as if she was going to pull it out. "You're not serious. But that means that everyone will know that I have a, a, a quirk!"

Zane finally figured it out. "Hush up, Dillon," he ordered. His ghostly nephew was obviously answering Akira's questions, and not carefully.

"This is terrible." Akira glared at him. She looked better when she was mad than when she was worried, he noted. That anxious look was gone, replaced by pink cheeks.

"Maybe not terrible," he tried. "Just maybe a little, um, inconvenient?"

"The research division is for scientists," Akira told him, as if he didn't know. "Special affairs is for psychics. And you run special affairs, and I work for you, which means that every person who knows that is going to know that I'm insane!"

"Or that we all are?" he offered. He really didn't want to make her any angrier but he was finding it hard not to smile at her scowling face. Maybe she was right that it was dangerous to be known as psychic in the outside world, but this was home, and no one here would think a thing of it. It just was what it was.

"You just don't get it," she snapped, gesturing widely with her hands. "Ghosts are dangerous! And—yes, all right, present company excepted—and—no, I'm sorry, Rose." She turned away from him. "I didn't mean to. . . No. Well, thank you. I appreciate that."

She threw an exasperated look over her shoulder at Zane. Rose? Everyone knew the Harris place was haunted, but that was the first time Zane had ever heard a name for the ghost. He made a mental note of it. He'd try to find out more later.

He could tell from Akira's posture and silence that she was listening to something he couldn't hear, but when she finally spoke the words weren't what he wanted to hear. "I should go home," she said, voice discouraged. "Back to California."

"Excuse me, Rose," Zane said hastily. Stepping forward, he grabbed Akira's hand, and tugged so she turned to face him again. "One month."

She just looked at him, dark eyes uncertain.

"One month," he repeated. "Give us one month. And if you have any problems here because of people believing you're psychic, we will help you find a job in a place where no one knows anything about you." Her fingers were cool in his, and he squeezed, trying to impart his own warmth to her.

This was a safe place.

He knew it was.

Now she just had to believe him.

~CHAPTER EIGHT~

Six weeks later

"Dillon, did you kill my Kindle again?" Akira tried to keep the accusation out of her voice. Maybe she'd forgotten to charge her e-reader. But she could tell from Dillon's sheepish look that she'd guessed right. She was sitting at a picnic table in a shady corner of General Direction's grounds, near the parking lot. "That's the third one! What am I supposed to do now? I wanted to read while I ate lunch."

"I'm sorry." He kicked the ground. "Rose was watching that ballroom dancing show, and it was really boring. But I'd been practicing. I thought maybe I'd gotten good enough to make it work."

Ever since Rose had discovered that she could zap the television remote to change the channels, Dillon had been trying to accomplish the same feat, although with less luck. Rose could apparently complete the circuit that changed the channels just as if someone had pressed a button. As long as the remote was positioned correctly—pointing at the television—she could control what they watched.

Akira had been both fascinated and relieved: getting woken up by a bored ghost who wanted her to find something new on the television had been the only part of living in a haunted house that she didn't like. Apart from Rose's television obsession, her ghostly housemates had proven to be good company. Henry sat with her while she ate breakfast every morning, peaceful and encouraging, never failing to tell her to enjoy her day when she headed out. The sound of the laughter from the boys in the backyard could make Akira smile in even her most anxious moments. And Rose and Dillon? Well, they were both so delighted with life—or afterlife—that their happiness was contagious.

Yes, living in a haunted house had turned out fine.

And General Directions was proving to be more than okay, too.

On her third day of work, Zane had stuck his head in her lab—her beautiful, sparkling, pristine lab with its digital oscilloscope, galvanometer, spectrometer, high-powered computer and other equipment—and said, "Come with me."

"You know, sonoluminescence could be caused by quantum vacuum radiation," Akira answered, not looking away from the numbers on her monitor. "The energy release might be too large, though."

"Um, yeah," Zane said. "Do you want to watch me work or not?"

"What?" That caught her attention and she turned her chair—her brand-new, comfortable, ergonomically-correct, fully-adjustable office chair—to look at him.

He grinned at her. "You wanted proof. I've got a DEA case that's only thirty miles away. Want to come?"

They'd met up with a frazzled-looking woman in a business-casual black jacket that didn't hide the shoulder holster underneath it. "We know the drugs got here," the woman told Zane. "But we can't find them. We've been searching for hours."

The house didn't look like Akira's idea of a drug den. It was probably no more than a couple of years old, a stucco-colored McMansion in a neighborhood that looked half-deserted. A surly Hispanic man was standing by a police car, hands cuffed behind his back. Akira watched as Zane went over and chatted with the man for a couple of minutes, touching his upper arm with a friendly pat, before returning to the woman. "You've got the wrong house," he told her.

"What?" Her shock was clear.

He nodded at a house two doors up the street. "Get a warrant for that place," he advised her.

"But we know the drugs arrived here, at this house," she insisted.

"Then look for the tunnel," he suggested with a shrug.

He and Akira waited. It was almost an hour before the new search warrant arrived, but it took Zane less than five minutes after that to find the drugs, along with a stash of assault weapons and some big bundles of cash, and the entrance to a tunnel that led straight back to the far corner of the first house's backyard.

Akira had been impressed. Also confused. The idea of a paranormal ability that let Zane find random objects as long as they were associated with a human being made no sense to her. "It must be some form of quantum entanglement," she finally told him, as they pulled into the parking lot of GD.

"Whatever you say." His tone was agreeable, but she suspected he was laughing at her.

She narrowed her eyes at him.

"Maybe you can research me after you finish with your sonoluminy-light-up-stuff," he offered with a grin.

She shook her head and sighed, but she couldn't help smiling.

That had been the beginning of a fun several weeks. She'd quickly settled into a routine. Most days, she read and researched in the morning, then had lunch with Dillon. Although GD had a nice cafeteria, more like a pleasant restaurant than a school lunchroom, Akira found it a little terrifying. It was often crowded and rooms full of strangers were not her favorite thing. Instead, she brought food from home and joined Dillon outside.

Max had offered her another car, so that Dillon's could stay parked anywhere that was comfortable for him, but Dillon had told Akira that he'd rather have some variety in his life, so he came with her to work most days. He'd managed to increase the range at which he could roam, but it took effort, so he usually hung out in the parking lot instead of following her into her lab.

At first, she'd found a pleasant spot under a tree next to the car. The sandy ground was dry, and sitting on it meant that she was mostly hidden from sight from people in the lot. She ate her lunch and talked to Dillon about the people she'd met and the work she was doing, and he told her more about his family, General Directions, and Tassamara.

During her second week at GD, though, she'd come outside to find Zane in her usual spot, leaning against a brand-new picnic table. "Is Dillon here?" he'd asked, without greeting her.

"Yes," she'd answered.

"Great," he'd said. "Ask him to tell you all about fire ants."

"Fire ants?"

"Yep."

She waited for more but he didn't seem to notice. He was turning a small package over in his hand, looking thoughtful.

"Okay, I will, thanks," Akira finally responded, still not sure what he was doing.

He looked up at her and his blue eyes caught hers. It was a beautiful day, sky clear, air cool, and in the bright sunlight, his eyes were bluer than usual. Akira felt her heart pick up its pace, just a little, and her cheeks start to pink at his direct stare. Damn, he was cute.

"Do you sit on the ground so that people won't see you?" he asked her, blunt and to the point.

"I—well—I—" Akira stumbled over her words, feeling defensive. And then she shrugged. "I don't like people thinking I'm talking to myself. I don't want . . ." She let her words trail off. How could she explain to him? She didn't want people talking about her. She was safer if no one noticed her.

"No one in Tassamara will think anything of it," he tried. "Lots of people here are . . ."

"Lunatics is the word you're looking for." Her voice was dry, but he smiled in response.

"Here." He tossed the package in her direction.

She caught it easily. "What is it?"

"Bluetooth headset. Wear it and talk all you like. People will just think you're on the phone."

And so her lunch routine had changed. Instead of sitting on the ground, at risk of fire ant attack, she sat at the picnic table, wearing a headset, and pretending she was on the phone when people walked by and eyed her. She wasn't sure which gift, the picnic table or the headset, was more thoughtful.

Since then, Zane had taken to showing up for lunch sometimes, too. Not always, not every day. But lately, most days. And if she was honest with herself, she could admit that they were the best days.

"I didn't think you were going to read at lunch," Dillon said. "Isn't Zane coming?"

"I don't know." Akira pulled out her phone and checked for messages. He hadn't texted her. Should she try him? You coming for lunch? she typed the text quickly, and then hit the send button, heart beating a little faster. She and Zane often exchanged texts—it seemed to be his favorite way of keeping in touch with people. But she usually just responded to his messages. This was the first time she'd ever initiated the exchange.

The response was almost immediate. You miss me?

A tiny smile curved her lips as Akira thought about how to answer that. Yes, was the truth. Was it too much truth? Dillon broke my Kindle, she typed.

Again?

That was too obvious to answer. Hmm. We need you to entertain us, she typed carefully, and then paused, finger over the send button, half-smiling but also chewing on her lower lip. Was that too blatant? Too suggestive? Zane had never asked her out, never been anything more than friendly. And he was her manager, ostensibly.

Not that he seemed to take his role all that seriously. Once, exasperated by the lack of structure, she'd asked him, "Do you even care if I work? Are you going to pay me if I just sit in my office all day?"

He'd grinned at her. "Yep. But you won't. You science types are terrible at entertaining yourselves." He'd been leaning back in his chair, feet up on his desk, tossing a nerf ball into the air and catching it on its way back down.

"I am not," she'd started defensively, before pausing and frowning. "What is that supposed to mean?"

"You'd get bored. Nobody gets a PhD in physics because they really love watching television."

Akira hadn't had a good answer for that, but it was true. She loved what she was working on. The freedom had its moments of terror—mornings when the whole day stretched in front of her, no classes, no students, no staff meetings—and what was she supposed to do? But she'd found a steady stream of answers. Although her work on sonoluminescence had been a total bust so far, she was busy writing a paper on the failures, and setting up for new experiments. And she had so many ideas she wanted to explore, so many experiments she could run, so much research she could read.

Still, Zane's role as her manager didn't seem as if it precluded a different kind of relationship. Not a serious one, of course: Akira didn't do serious. Not when even her casual relationships burned out fast. It was amazing how quickly guys could move on when they found out she could see ghosts, or thought she could.

But Zane already knew about the ghosts. And oh, he was cute. Those blue eyes, the grin, the muscles, the lean hands . . . she really liked his hands. She'd spent more than a pleasant minute or two imagining them touching her.

"Are you flirting with my uncle?"

Akira hit the send button. Then she looked at Dillon, who had crossed his arms and was frowning at her. "Got a problem with that?" she asked. She might be sharing her life with ghosts these days, but she was not going to let them think they could push her around. She might have wimped out on sending that text, but not if Dillon disapproved.

He uncrossed his arms. "I guess not." He shrugged. "But, um . . . my uncle's kind of . . . well, he's had a lot of girlfriends."

Ah. Dillon wasn't warning her off, he was worrying about her. That was unexpectedly sweet. He was a bit of a worrier, though. He warned her about how fast she drove, the preservatives in her food, emissions from her cell phone.

Akira had never asked him about his death, because it wasn't always a safe topic with ghosts, but she did wonder how such a cautious kid had wound up overdosing. Maybe he'd been more of a risk-taker before he died.

"Thank you," she answered, before smiling at him. "Don't worry, I'm not a happy-ever-after type. I won't start any great romantic fantasies about him."

Her phone shivered in her hand. She looked down. Wish I could. Trapped in meetings.

Darn. The pang of disappointment she felt was too strong. Casual flirtation, she reminded herself. That's all she was doing. Nothing to feel disappointed about.

Need to see you, though. My office, 4PM.

Hmm, that sounded almost formal.

Need, not want? Akira wondered. Suddenly that little glimmer of anticipation was gone, replaced by a twinge of anxiety.

OK, she typed. Should she ask what about?

See you then. His reply came too fast, and sounded too final. With a frown, Akira slid her phone back into her bag. She and Dillon would just have to lunch alone.

And while she ate, Dillon could fill her in on Zane's past girlfriends.

❧

"Nothing."

It was 4:02 PM, and Akira was standing in the doorway of Zane's office, unsure whether to interrupt. Grace was perched on the edge of his desk, her back to the door, blocking Zane from view.

"Try again," Grace ordered.

"Grace, nothing means nothing." Zane sounded both resigned and impatient.

Grace sighed and stood, tucking a piece of paper, maybe a photograph, Akira thought, into a file folder. "Do you want her to come here or do you want to go there?"

"Neither."

"Lucas took the job, Zane. It's done. You just have to do it."

"Or not," Zane grumbled, before adding, "Talk to them, tell them how unlikely it is that I can help. If they still want me, I'll fly up there tomorrow. And tell Lucas that his next job is going to be in Antarctica."

Grace reached over and rumpled his hair, saying with a smile, "Lucas would love to go to Antarctica, sweetie. You're going to do have to do better than that."

Zane pulled away from her. "I hate jobs like this, Grace. Tell Lucas—oh, hey, Akira." His motion had been enough to bring him into her line of view. Akira gave him a tentative smile.

Grace glanced over her shoulder, spotting Akira, and immediately turned and crossed toward the doorway. "I'll let you know, but you know they're going to want to see you. Hi, Akira."

Akira dipped her chin, acknowledging Grace's greeting, but feeling awkward about having interrupted them. "If you're busy, I can come back later," she offered.

She had been surprised to discover that Grace was Zane's sister: the blonde woman looked nothing like her siblings. She'd been even more surprised to learn that the woman she'd assumed was a receptionist on her first day was actually the CEO of the business, managing day-to-day operations since Max retired. Max was still involved as Chairman of the Board, but Zane and Smithson—the heads of special affairs and research, respectively—reported to Grace. Dillon claimed that she sat at the front desk sometimes because it was how she started and she still liked it.

"We're not," Zane sounded grim, but Grace also shook her head.

Reaching the doorway, she said quietly, so that only Akira could hear, "Cheer him up if you can. Tomorrow's going to be a rough day."

Akira glanced at her quickly. What did that mean? What did Grace expect? But the blonde woman just squeezed her arm in passing and continued out of the room. Akira stepped into Zane's office. He was rubbing his forehead, looking tired.

"Um, do you still want to see me?" she asked. Should she be here? Grace's orders to cheer him up notwithstanding, he didn't look as if he wanted company.

He looked up at her and smiled, but it was strained. "Did I—oh!" It was as if a realization had struck, and his smile turned into a full-fledged grin. "Yes, I do want to see you." He waved at the space behind her. "Check it out."

Akira looked. The first time she'd visited the playroom Zane called an office, Akira had laughed aloud. It made so much more sense than the barren cell he'd used for her interview.

On the fourth floor, it was a large L-shaped room that might have been intended to be a conference room, or—if the complex had been built as a private school, as she suspected—a combination science lab/classroom. Zane, however, had turned one leg of the L into an arcade, with six old video games, a foosball table, and an air hockey table. The second leg of the L was a living room, with a comfortable couch, a couple of easy chairs, a huge flat-screen television on the wall, and more video game consoles than she knew the names of. Only the corner of the L looked like an office, with a desk, chairs, office equipment, even file cabinets.

Now, though, in the space that she thought of as the arcade, the foosball table and the air hockey table were gone, replaced by a pool table. And not a trivial pool table—a real one, with ornate carved legs, a mahogany finish, rich green felt—the type of pool table that cost thousands of dollars. Her eyes widened.

"A pool table?" she asked. "That's why you wanted to meet with me?"

"Yep." A slightly sheepish expression crossed his face. "I guess I could have waited for next week at our usual time."

Zane met with all the employees of the special affairs division one-on-one, once a week, to assign new jobs, get updated on the progress of their current jobs, talk about any problems, and so on. Officially, that was. Based on her meetings with him, Akira thought that meant he probably spent a lot of time playing foosball or Halo.

"But what happened to foosball? I thought you loved foosball."

"I decided it was time for a change," he answered, standing and moving out from behind his desk. He paused next to her, their shoulders almost brushing, and she looked up at him. He was admiring the table, his smile still playing around his mouth, but he looked down at her as if he felt her gaze, and his lips quirked. "And you did say you'd play pool."

"I did?" she questioned. "When did I say that?"

Every time they met, he tried to convince her to play some game: foosball first, but then usually a video game. And every time, she declined. She'd been trying to keep their meetings professional. Lately, though, as their relationship slipped over the line into personal anyway, it had been getting harder to resist. At their last meeting, she'd been laughing when she said no to bowling on the Kinect.

"It was when you got all huffy about Ms. Pac-Man."

Akira thought back. That had been weeks ago. "Huffy? Just because I told you it was sexist to think I'd like Ms. Pac-Man better than Halo?" The words might have sounded challenging, but he'd be able to hear the smile in her voice.

"Grace does, Nat does. I wasn't being sexist, just generalizing from experience," he defended himself mildly, crossing to the rack of pool cues. "And if you remember, you said . . ."

"I said that girls might like Ms. Pac-Man, but that physicists like pool," Akira interrupted him, joining him by the rack and eying the cues, before picking up one that looked about right. She hefted it carefully, checking its weight and grip before putting it back on the rack and picking up another one. "I remember."

"Does this mean you're going to play pool with me?"

"Oh, yeah," Akira answered, lashes down, covering her eyes. "Eight-ball work for you? Call shot, open break?"

Yes, she was definitely going to play pool with him. And not just pool. The sizzle running through her veins told her that her impulsive streak—the one that brought her to Tassamara in the first place—had just made a decision.

The only question left was how direct she was going to be about acting on that decision. And she thought maybe the answer was very direct. Cheer him up? Yeah, she could do that.

Zane didn't know it yet but their casual flirtation had just been upgraded.

❧

Zane had been happier about finally finding a game that Akira would play before she killed him six games in a row.

"Best, um, seven out of thirteen?" he offered, leaning against the pool table with a sigh. She laughed. She'd taken off her light sweater a while back, revealing a black tank top, and he wished he could blame all of his losses on the distraction her dark curls brushing against her almost bare shoulders had caused him, but when it came to pool, she was out of his league. She'd even let him break that time, but it made no difference. "Or maybe some Halo?"

"You ready to start shooting me?" she asked, a half smile curving her lips as she finished racking the balls.

"Only virtually," he drawled. Actually, shooting her wouldn't be his first choice. Watching the way she moved around the table for the past hour, the concentration on her face, the graceful way she held the cue—and oh, hell, yeah, the curve of her ass as she bent to make a shot, the shadow down the neckline of her shirt—he really wanted to touch her. To taste her. To lift her up onto the edge of the table and take her lips and feel her legs wrap around him and pull him close.

But he knew he couldn't rush her. She was wary and cautious and even though he'd kept Max away from her, refusing to allow him to try to pressure her into communicating with his dead, Zane still wasn't sure she wouldn't just run away one day.

"Physicists ought to be good at Halo, too," he pointed out. "Pool isn't the only game where angles matter."

"Oh, pool definitely isn't the only game physicists are good at," Akira replied, placing her cue back in the rack.

"Oh, yeah? What other games do physicists like?" He was watching her, more attention on her legs than on her words, trying to imagine what they looked like under her pants, what they'd feel like if he could touch them.

"Sex."

He blinked, eyes shooting up to her face. Had she just said that?

"Chemists think it's all about chemistry," she said, crossing to him, taking the pool cue out of his hand, taking it back to the rack and putting it away, then returning, even as she continued talking. Her words were casual, conversational, but there was a hint of breathlessness in her voice that told him they were more than theoretical.

"Hormones and pheromones. Some peptides, a little oxytocin, vasopressin, and that's the whole story. But what do they know? Really, sex is all about physics."

She was standing in front of him, looking up at him, and whatever she saw on his face, it was right, because she took his hand and with a little smile, started tugging him with her to the other side of the room.

He followed, saying huskily, "I don't know. The chemistry seems to be working fine for me." His jeans were abruptly feeling constricting, as she pushed him down onto the brown leather couch.

"That's because we haven't started playing with physics yet." She retreated to the office door, and locked it, then turned back to face him. "You have no professional objections to playing my game in your office, do you?"

The mischief in her smile told him that she knew exactly how unlikely that was. "Not in the least," he assured her.

"Oh, but—" she paused and bit her lip.

No, no, no, he thought fervently. Don't change your mind. The attraction he'd felt the day they'd met had deepened over the past weeks: something about her mix of fragility and determination, her stubborn fearfulness, caught him like no one else ever had. He wanted to tease her, to protect her, and to make love to her, sometimes all at the same time.

"I didn't really come prepared for, um, this type of game," she continued. "Are you—do you—would you happen to have . . . ?" She tucked her hair behind her ear and tilted her head to the side, looking at him as if hoping he'd read her mind, her cheeks turning slightly pink. "My game requires approved protective gear."

Oh, hell. He tried to remember if he'd ever had a reason to bring condoms to work and then realized that the travel kit he kept in his desk for quick trips might be stocked. Standing, he crossed to his desk, opened the bottom drawer, found his bag, and rummaged through it, all the while acutely aware of her eyes on him, and of his heart racing. Ah, there.

Holding up the foil wrapper, he said, "Is this what you're looking for?"

She smiled at him demurely, and his fingers tightened on the wrapper as he felt his body respond with a surge of pure lust. "Exactly."

She gestured with her head toward the couch and he met her in front of it, dropping the condom onto the end table, as she placed one small hand on his chest. "So what's wrong with chemistry?" he asked in a murmur, bending his head toward her, intending to kiss her, until she put a finger up and across his lips.

"Not a thing," she said. "But physics is better." He let her hold him off, waiting to see where she was going.

"See, physics is about touch, and then movement," she said, not looking him in the face. She slid her hands over his shirt, and then, one at a time, carefully, slowly, she opened the buttons, as she started to stroke, tracing patterns into his chest, circling her fingers delicately around his nipples and then tracing away, down, down, and then back up again.

She looked up at him, eyes glinting with humor, and he realized that she knew exactly what she was doing to him. "I could tell you all about your sensory system, the way your neurons are transmitting electrical impulses, the ions breaking through the cell walls, but we'll just focus on friction for the moment."

"Friction, huh?" He shrugged out of his shirt, letting it drop onto the ground behind him, and then brought his hands to rest on her hips, pulling her a little closer so that he could feel her soft curves. She wiggled against him, just a little, and he closed his eyes, trying to resist the need to go faster. Much, much faster. But he took a deep breath, and let his hands slide up and under her tank top, touching the warmth of her bare skin as she continued.

"Friction," she said, moving her hands up his chest, "is the force that resists the motion of two surfaces against one another. Too much friction is a bad thing, of course, but just the right amount of friction . . ."

Her hands were stroking, caressing, around his back and down, over his jeans, and then back up, pulling his head down to hers.

He followed her lead, reaching down to let her take his mouth with hers, letting his lips open under her searching tongue until he couldn't resist any longer and began exploring, caressing the soft skin of her lips with his mouth until her head fell back and she let him nibble and stroke his way along her chin and down the taut line of her neck.

"Just the right amount of friction," she continued breathlessly, ". . . and kinetic energy gets converted to heat."

"Oh, yeah, I think that's definitely happening here," Zane murmured against her skin.

"Mmm." Her response was wordless, before she took a step back. He let her go reluctantly, but she just smiled, reaching down to the base of her tank top and pulling it smoothly over her head. He closed his eyes, almost in pain at the sight of the black lace bra and her gentle curves, but she was already reaching around herself, unhooking the bra and letting it fall to the ground.

She looped a finger in the top of his jeans and pulled him toward her. "May I?"

"God, yes."

She laughed, and unbuttoned the first button on his jeans, but then paused. "Maybe we should skip ahead?"

"To?" He reached for the clasp on her slacks, and slipped it free, then pushed the sides off her hips, letting her pants fall to the ground. She stepped out of them and kicked them aside, then stood there, eyes dreamy and thoughtful, dressed only in black silk panties with lace around the edge, and black heels. Her skin was pale and lovely, her dark curls falling around her shoulders, her pupils dark and dilated, and skipping ahead sounded like a really good plan to him. He wanted to bury himself in her, to feel her wrapping herself around him, and every moment he had to wait was a slow torture.

"Oscillation is always nice," she murmured, still motionless. "You know what oscillation is, right?"

"Movement?" He used his toes on his heels to pull his shoes off without bending down, then shoved them under the couch with his foot, before moving his hands over hers and starting to help with his own buttons.

"Not just movement. A repetitive variation around a point." As he let his jeans drop, her hand closed around his warmth. He reached for her as she added, "I bet you can find a really good place to oscillate."

"Oh, God," he groaned, taking her mouth, his hands tangling in her hair as he kissed her, deep, intense, greedy, vitally aware of her hand tight around his hardness, the warmth of her curves so close to him. "I never knew physics was so fascinating."

She laughed and dropped backward onto the couch, pulling him down with her. He explored her body, touching and tasting her, until oscillation became irresistible, when he reached for the condom.

He paused, fighting for control. "Science class was not like this."

"Shall I tell you about resonant frequencies?" she whispered, stroking her hands down his back, as he slid inside her.

"It can't be better than oscillation," he answered, as he started to move. She felt amazing, so hot, so soft, and he wanted it to last forever. But he also wanted to move, faster, and faster, and to feel her moving with him.

"Oh, but it is," she said, breathlessly, arching underneath him. "Physical systems have frequencies." She ended with a gasp as he stroked his hand up her body, cupping her breast, thumbing the taut nipple.

"Mmm-hmm," he murmured, letting his voice ask the question.

"Frequencies at which they vibrate. Hit the right frequency . . . the resonant frequency . . . and an amplitude disturbance . . . reinforces the energy stored in the system."

He had no idea what she was talking about. Absolutely none. But he loved her gasping voice, the husky breathiness, and the way her body was responding to his. He moved a little faster, feeling how close he was to the edge, but wanting to make it last, wanting to bring her with him.

"Resonant frequencies make music. Shatter glass. Make bridges collapse. And—ohhh." He could feel her contracting around him and that was it, that was enough, that was too much, and he let go, feeling himself exploding inside her.

"Yeah, that, too," she murmured.

☙CHAPTER NINE❧

The post-orgasmic bliss lasted two or three minutes—not bad for Akira. The post-sex anxiety started immediately thereafter.

Shit. She'd slept with her boss. And not just slept with him, seduced him. Hell, she hadn't even made him buy her dinner first. And that third date rule? Smashed to bits.

But he'd bought her a pool table, she reminded herself. Oh, not as a gift, of course, but she knew that pool table was here so that she would play with him. A small smile crept across her face, and she turned her head, letting her lips brush across his bare shoulder. His arm tightened around her.

They were still lying on the couch, still tangled together. Zane had gotten up briefly, then returned, shifting so that she was half on top of him, tucked into the secure side of the couch, her back pressing against its back.

"So," Zane murmured. "How did you get so good at pool?"

Pool, huh? That was what he was interested in? Well, it was what she'd been thinking about, too. "Practice, practice, practice and . . ."

"Let me guess, more practice."

"We had a pool table in the house. My dad and I played a lot. Almost every day before he got really sick."

Zane stroked his hand down her back, a touch that felt sympathetic, not sexual, but before he could say anything else, his phone buzzed. There was a mutual pause, a hesitation born of uncertainty. Would they let the interruption break the moment? And then Akira moved, shifting off Zane and away, so that he could get up. With a resigned sigh, he swung his legs off the couch and reached for his jeans. As he dug out his phone, she gathered up her clothes, and quickly began to dress.

"Damn it," he muttered as he read his incoming text.

"Bad news?"

"You could say that," he agreed, not looking up from his phone as he one-handedly typed a response.

Akira pulled her tank top over her head and looked around for her sweater. Where had she left it? Ah, right, across the room, draped over the Asteroids cabinet. She grabbed it, but didn't slip it on, clutching it in her hand as she returned to the couch. "Well, I'll just leave you to it, I guess."

"No, no, no," Zane said, springing to his feet, and stepping closer to her.

"No?" Akira asked the question lightly, smiling, trying not to let the trickle of relief she felt at his words show on her face. Navigating the territory between flirtation, casual sex, friends with benefits, or something more was so damn hard. It wasn't that she had any expectations: she'd acted on an impulse, and if it was only a fun evening, well, it had still been fun. But it was nice that he didn't want her to leave. Maybe more than nice.

"No," he repeated firmly. He hadn't put on any clothes yet, but he didn't seem at all self-conscious about his nudity as he took her hand and tugged her closer, lifting her hand to his mouth and pressing his lips against her knuckles, before dropping it and sliding his hand around the nape of her neck. She swayed into him, feeling the liquid warmth starting again, the tingle of attraction running through her veins. Leaning down so that his lips were only a few inches away from hers, he added huskily, "A good teacher should never leave her pupils confused."

"Confused?" Akira breathed the question, eyes on his mouth.

"I'm a very bad physics student," he confessed. "You completely lost me at amplitudes."

"Oh, I don't know," she said, reaching up to take his lips. She let the kiss last, long, and slow, and deep, before pulling back and saying breathlessly, "I think you have a natural talent."

"Um, Akira?"

Akira's eyes widened and she stepped back from Zane. "Dillon? What are you doing here?"

"Not looking," Dillon responded, voice dry, as Zane's eyebrows shot up. Akira nodded at Zane, confirming that yes, his 15-year-old ghostly nephew was in the room.

She was grateful to be wearing her clothes—and that Dillon hadn't shown up ten minutes earlier—as Zane, without rushing, grabbed his jeans and underwear and started dressing. "Nice timing, Dill," he drawled. "I didn't know you could reach my office."

"It took some effort," Dillon said. "And it's not comfortable. I feel like I'm being stretched like saltwater taffy. But it's late."

"What's he saying?" Zane asked, pulling on his t-shirt.

Akira shook her head, not wanting to get into explanations. "We played pool for a while, and it's getting late. I should go."

"Take Dillon home," Zane suggested. "I'll pick you up there and we can go out to dinner. In my car. And then we'll figure out where we can pick up our physics lesson without interruption. I moved back in with my dad and Grace after my mom died, so how do you feel about—yeah, I thought not," he finished, seeing her shaking her head before he'd made it through the question. No way was she sleeping with him in the same house as the CEO and Chairman of the Board of the company she worked for. Maybe they were his relatives, but they signed her paycheck. "Your house?"

Akira thought for a moment. She still had a pleasant little rush of desire running through her. And she wanted to spend more time with Zane. Plus, if she started letting her ghostly companions limit her activities, where would she stop? She nodded. "I'll have a little conversation with my, um, roommates, about boundaries and privacy first."

"Hey, I can't exactly knock, you know," Dillon answered as Zane grinned at her. "I got worried. I'm still worried," he added pointedly.

Akira gave him an exasperated look. They'd had this conversation over lunch. Dillon thought his uncle was going to break her heart. And even though he hadn't said so, he was undoubtedly worried about the consequences for him if Zane did. But Akira wasn't afraid. Her heart was tough, and her walls were thick. After a lifetime of keeping secrets and a few failed relationships, she knew better than to count on other people. Even other people who bought pool tables so that she'd play with them. "I'm fine," she told him.

"I've been watching a lot of television," Dillon told her. "These things don't end well."

"What're you and Rose watching?" Akira asked. "Soap operas?"

"It's some show about housewives. People keep on dying. And relationships all end badly."

Akira smiled at him. She and Zane were just going to have a little fun: there would be nothing desperate about it.

"Hey, do you want to come to North Carolina with me?"

He was a morning person. She could hear it in his voice, all cheerful and wide-awake despite how little sleep they'd had. Damn. Morning people, blah. She opened a reluctant eye, and peered at the clock. 7:47.

"Why are you awake?" she muttered, finishing with a yawn that she buried in her pillow.

"Because it's morning?" he offered in response, before tugging lightly on a lock of her dark hair. "Come on, come to North Carolina with me."

She rolled over, onto her back, and stretched, arms above her head, back arching, and then wiggled down in the bed, a little deeper under the light sheet that covered her. Hmm. Even half-awake, she could see his reaction to her movement in the way his eyes darkened, the lids half dropping. "Or you could come back to bed," she suggested, voice husky with sleep.

"The body is so, so willing," he said, sliding his hand across her stomach and leaning down to kiss her. "But the brain is stuck with responsibility," he added as he sat back up, mouth twisting.

"In North Carolina?" Akira asked, reluctantly sitting up, sheet clutched high.

"Yeah, Lucas . . ." Zane shook his head, apparently not wanting to get into details, but looking grim. "He took a job for me."

"A job?" Akira was surprised. Zane might play a lot of foosball at work, but she'd gathered that he was the one who coordinated assignments for the people whose work involved . . . quirks. Didn't he usually give Lucas jobs? "Isn't that backwards?"

Zane sighed. "Yeah, but the only reason Lucas works for me instead of the other way around is that he doesn't do so well staying home. He's not an office type."

Akira bit back her smile, but Zane obviously saw it, because he grinned at her and trailed a finger down her cheek, before saying, "He doesn't know what he's missing."

"I was just thinking that your office isn't very—um, formal," she defended herself. She hadn't been thinking about what they'd done in his office, just that Zane didn't seem to draw the lines between work and play that most people did.

"Yeah, well, Lucas likes the road. But a lot of the work we do comes from his connections. Whoever asked him to do this job probably knew I'd say no. Someone's calling in a favor." Zane stood with a sigh. He was already showered and half-dressed, Akira realized.

That sounded so dubious, she thought. Favors? Were they the Mafia? "You don't know who you're working for?" she asked. She was feeling an unwieldy mix of doubt and curiosity, a combination of uncertainty about who Zane was and what he did and a desire to know more.

"That sounds a lot more exciting than it really is." Zane was looking around for his t-shirt. "It'll be someone in the FBI."

"The FBI?" That was better than the mob, but not necessarily less exciting.

"Yeah." Zane pulled on his shirt. "So, you want to come?"

"Is anyone going to be shooting at you?" Akira asked, not sure what she'd do if the answer was yes. Briefly, she remembered what Grace had said the day before about today being a rough day.

"I wish," Zane answered, almost as if to himself. "It'd be more fun."

Her eyebrows arched up. Had Grace been understating? What was wrong with this job Zane was doing? What exactly was he going to do? She didn't say anything but he looked back at her, and must have seen the questions as he tried to smile. "No, it's just a straightforward job. I'm going to fly up there in the company plane, meet Lucas at the airport, hold someone's hand for five minutes, tell her I can't find what she's looking for, and then fly home. No big deal, really."

He sat down on the edge of the bed again. She was sitting, the sheet tucked around her body, one hand under her chin, and he brushed her hair back, off her shoulder. "So, no go?"

"Are you kidding?" Akira smiled at him. She didn't understand what was going on. She was definitely missing something. But she wanted to find out what it was, and there was an easy way to do so. "A chance to spend the day above the clouds in a little tin can that bounces around like a carnival ride?" She leaned forward and brushed a kiss across his lips. "Do I have time to shower?"

The pilot was a surprise. He was the tow-truck driver from Akira's car accident of several weeks earlier.

"You fly planes and drive tow-trucks?" Akira glanced at Zane uncertainly but he was busy filling out paperwork at the tiny airport's front desk.

Dave grinned at her. "Drive one buggy, you can drive 'em all," he assured her.

That was why he'd seemed familiar before, she realized: he was the pilot who had flown her to Tassamara on her very first visit. He'd been wearing a baseball cap and sunglasses, and she'd been so nervous at first that she hadn't remembered his face.

"Dave used to fly the space shuttle," Zane drawled from behind her. "A little plane like this is nothing to him."

Was Zane teasing? Akira looked at Dave and he shrugged. "Not a lot of jobs with NASA anymore."

Akira wasn't sure whether it was reassuring or not to know that the pilot had flown in space, but she didn't say a word when he handed control over to Zane and let him bring them most of the way to North Carolina. She could see Zane's hands on the controls from her forward-facing seat behind the pilot, and between the soothing sound of the engines, the lack of sleep, and the smooth flight in clear blue skies, she spent most of the trip in a pleasant half-daydream, half-doze, thinking about the way those hands had touched her, and how they felt on her skin.

At the airport, however, there was no Lucas, just a car with a driver.

"Oh, hell," muttered Zane. "I'm going to kill Lucas." He strode across the tarmac toward the car as Akira and Dave followed him out of the plane.

"So," Dave said to Akira, voice casual, as they watched Zane's back receding. "Ghosts, huh?"

Akira glanced at him and frowned. It had been weeks since their first encounter: why were ghosts still on his mind?

"You should go with him." Dave wasn't looking at her and his tone was unrevealing.

"Why's that?" Akira asked warily.

"I need to stay with the plane, and he could use the company."

Akira's frown deepened. Did that have something to do with ghosts?

The pilot looked at her and smiled, a twist of his lips that didn't reach his eyes. "You might be able to help him."

"How so?" Akira asked.

"Grace let me know when she called to schedule the flight that it was a lost kid case. If the kid was alive, Zane would know where he is already."

Oh, hell. Had Zane brought her here thinking she'd talk to a ghost for him? The stab of pain was almost physical; the betrayal a bitter taste in her mouth. And then she looked at Zane, leaning down and talking to the driver of the car, and bit her lip.

She'd go with him. She'd see what this was. And if he had been manipulating her—well, she'd deal with that when she was sure it was true.

~

The drive was quiet.

Akira was silent, gazing out the window without noticing the scenery, trying to remember every shade, every nuance, of the conversations that had brought her here. Zane hadn't mentioned ghosts. Or lost children, for that matter. But he hadn't tried to persuade her to come, either. No promises of fun and excitement, no words that turned on the charm.

But had he lied to her? Had he known that Lucas wouldn't meet them? She didn't think so, but she wasn't sure.

She sighed.

Zane was texting, but he put his hand over hers, where it lay in her lap, for a quick squeeze, before bringing it back to his smart phone. "I'm sorry about this," he said, not really turning his attention to her. "Lucas is saying that circumstances have changed, but he's not giving me a lot of information. I'm still not sure what's happened."

Akira glanced at his phone. Surely it would be faster for him to just call and talk to Lucas? Was he texting so that she wouldn't overhear what he said? She glanced at his face, his profile turned to her, trying to reconcile her paranoid thoughts with the man she thought she'd come to know.

She couldn't.

She liked him, she really did, and seeing him as a liar and a manipulator just didn't fit. Dillon's warnings about his uncle had been about girlfriends, casual relationships, a lack of commitment coupled with a playful attitude toward life, not lies. She was ready to be stood up when a baseball game called, not to be deceived about ulterior motives. Zane just didn't seem like an ulterior motive kind of guy.

His phone buzzed. "Oh, hell," he muttered as he read his message. He glanced at her quickly, almost as if to check whether she was reading over his shoulder, and then grimaced when he saw that she was watching him. "You're not going to like this."

She raised her eyebrows in the question, but didn't say anything. She could feel her shoulders tensing. Was he going to ask her about ghosts?

He looked worried, eyes tightening. "This was a custody case: the dad took his kid and disappeared. Happens all the time, and mostly the kids wind up home within a few days. But this dad is gone, gone. No one's seen him, his car, anything. He hasn't used any of his credit cards or taken money out of any banks. Best-case scenario would be that he spent a long time planning this."

"And worst-case?" Akira asked the question even though she already knew the answer.

"That's what the feds think it is, now." Zane sighed.

"You brought me to the scene of a murder-suicide?" Akira couldn't keep the accusation—and maybe the hurt—out of her voice. He had to know what that meant. They hadn't talked much about the ghosts. Oh, sure, he'd asked her a few questions over the past several weeks, but mostly about Dillon. He seemed to respect her wish to not talk about what she could see. But even though Akira knew that a lot of the common stories about ghosts were wrong, Zane had to suspect that a murder-suicide was likely to leave ghost energy behind.

Zane's eyes widened. "No," he protested. "Definitely not! We're going to the mom's house, and there's no way anyone died there."

Damn. Maybe they should have had a few more conversations about ghosts. Ghosts weren't always tied to the place they died. Some were, but not all of them.

"No," Zane continued. "The problem is—the thing is—see, what's happened is—"

The car had slowed dramatically and Akira, looking over Zane's shoulder, could see the reason why. "The media found out?" she offered Zane. "And let me guess—the kid is cute?"

Following her glance, he saw what she was looking at. Cars. Lots of cars. And vans. The ones with satellite dishes on their roofs. Flashing lights from police cars, people milling around, reporters directing cameras, a crowd of neighbors, and behind it all, a driveway leading up to a posh, Palladian suburban house with a lopsided "For Sale" sign planted in the lush grass of the front yard.

"I'm so sorry," Zane apologized. "If Lucas had told me, I wouldn't have asked you to come."

"I'll wait in the car," Akira said, looking past the crowd to the house. It was definitely haunted. She could see the shimmers of energy, almost like a color change in the air near the door of the house. It wasn't just a ghost, it was a fresh ghost with a lot of power. Maybe a desperate ghost. That made it dangerous for her.

"I'm sorry, ma'am." The driver, in the front seat, had been listening to the conversation. "I'm only supposed to drop you off. The other Mr. Latimer will be driving you back to the airport. I've got to get back to work."

"Can you take her back to the airport first?" Zane interjected.

"No can-do, sorry." The driver's words were firm.

Zane looked at Akira. "Do you want to wait outside? I can find Lucas, and make him arrange for another car."

Akira looked at the crowds of newspeople, already eagerly motioning toward their car. "Oh, that's just a thrilling idea," she said bitterly.

"I'm sorry," Zane repeated, but a little less apologetically than he had the first time. "If I had known, I wouldn't have brought you. But I didn't. This should only take a few minutes."

A few minutes. Depending on how perceptive the ghost was, that could be bad. But Akira looked at Zane's face, his expression anxious but firm, and knew that he hadn't lied to her. He didn't understand the risks, but he hadn't lied.

"I'll come inside," she said. They'd have a long talk after this. She'd tell him some of what she knew about ghosts. After that, if past experience held true, she probably wouldn't be sleeping with him again.

Damn.

Today was turning into a day when she should have stayed in bed.

☙CHAPTER TEN❧

Lucas was an older, tougher, more heavily muscled, more serious version of Zane. They were clearly brothers, but on Lucas, the charm held an edge of danger.

Akira managed not to glare at him, simply smiling tightly as they were introduced. Inwardly, though, she was thinking, Asshole. Damn him for putting her in this situation.

But her eyes narrowed as she saw him rubbing his temple with a wince of pain, as he responded wryly, "It's a pleasure to meet you, too." Huh. Did Lucas, like the others in his family, have a psychic gift? But she dismissed the thought as he ushered them through the foyer, past the formal living room, and down a hallway to a more casual but still luxurious family room.

The room held half a dozen people and one very upset ghost. Akira dropped her eyes to the ground on an intake of breath. Shit. The ghost was kneeling by a blonde woman who was sitting at the edge of a plush recliner, her face buried in her hands as if she was too tired, too overwhelmed to hold her head up. He had the flickering, flaring edges of passion, as if his form couldn't contain his energy.

But it was only tinted a pale red, Akira reassured herself, stealing another glance. Barely pink. That meant that his consciousness, such as it was, was still in control. But murder-suicide? And of a child? It might not matter that the ghost was able to control himself if he didn't choose to. She could feel her heart beating faster, a pulse pounding in her neck.

No one here knew anything, she realized. No one would be able to help her if the ghost attacked. Abruptly, and for the first time in years, she longed for her father.

A warm hand slid into hers, and squeezed. "Okay?" Zane asked, tone quiet so that only she could hear, eyes intent on her face.

She tried to smile at him, but she couldn't quite manage it.

He didn't understand, she knew. It wasn't just the ghost: if he knew there was a ghost here, he would think of Dillon or Rose, and not see the problem. But ghost energy was like other energy—and a shock from an electric outlet didn't compare to getting hit by lightning, a fire in a fireplace was nothing like a burning house.

"I'll try to make this quick, but—" He looked in the direction of the blonde woman and even though Akira didn't want to take any chance of the ghost seeing her, she followed his gaze. The woman had lifted her head and the tear stains tracking down her face, the red eyes, the exhaustion were all obvious, even from across the room.

Akira bit her lip. The woman had lost a child. Zane was her chance of finding him, or at least finding answers. He shouldn't make it quick, he should take as long as he needed to be sure. She pressed her lips together, but said steadily, "I'll be fine. Take your time." She hoped her words were true.

He let go of her hand, stroking up her back and resting his hand on her neck for just a second or two, then nodding at her and moving away, crossing the room to where Lucas was standing, almost on top of the ghost.

Akira turned away. A sliding glass door led to a patio, and she crossed to it, not really looking, trying to think through her options if the ghost discovered her.

A quick escape? But if he hadn't died here, he probably wasn't tied here. She wouldn't be able to get away from him so easily.

She rested her hand on the door pull anyway, feeling the comfort of the cool metal under her hand. There were plenty of people in the room, she reminded herself, and no reason for the ghost to single her out. As long as she didn't pay attention to him, he wouldn't pay attention to her. It would be okay, really it would.

And then her eyes narrowed. Oh, dear.

She glanced back at Zane. The blonde had stood and was shaking hands with him, an uncertain hope on her face. Akira bit her lip and looked back out into the yard.

And then, with a sigh, she flipped open the lock on the door and stepped outside.

She tried to feel resolute, but really, she was mostly just hoping she didn't wind up regretting what she was about to do.

◈

Lucas introduced Zane to the mother, but Zane promptly forgot her name. He didn't want to remember. He just wanted to get through this and get out of here.

Lost kid cases could be amazing. Once, he'd located a toddler, who'd wandered away from home, in a drainage ditch almost two miles away. Another time, he'd found a kidnapped girl, alive and well and scared out of her wits, in the trunk of a car. Those were fun.

Mostly, though, lost kid cases sucked. Big-time. Sure, it was nice to show up and be a hero, but it didn't usually work that way. Even custody cases, where the child was almost always alive and well, sometimes left him feeling queasy. He'd helped find and return a little girl to a dad with sole custody once and the desperation in the mom's eyes kept him awake at night for months afterwards.

And this time, he already knew. The absolute flat nothing he felt when he touched the photo of the beautiful blond toddler meant the boy was dead. When he touched a photo of a living person, he almost always got something—oh, maybe not something very clear—but something. A sense of distance, if the person was far away; a sense of light and color and surroundings, if the person was nearer; an absolute knowledge of place if the person was close by. Touching something that belonged to the person improved his range, touching hair or blood or something with DNA improved it further. In this case, though, it would make no difference and the hope on the mother's face was almost painful.

Really, insurance cases were just so much better. Why couldn't he just find some missing jewels? A nice painting? Hardly anybody ever cried about stolen goods.

"Let's sit down on the couch," Zane suggested to the blonde. "Before we start, I need you to know that I don't think I'm going to be able to help you."

"Your brother's said that already." The woman nodded and tried to muster a smile. "But I'll try anything." Her eyes filled with tears, and she blinked them back. Zane tried to hide his wince. Damn it. If Lucas had just brought her to the airport, he could have been done with this and out of here already.

As they sat down, he continued, trying to be soothing without sounding hopeful. "What I'll do is hold your hand for a while and see if I feel anything. With objects, I have a better range when I'm touching the person who owns the object, and that sometimes helps with missing family members, too."

"If he can't find Daniel," Lucas interjected. "He'll try to find Rob, the car, their clothes, anything we can think of that Rob might have with him."

'Oh, fuck you,' Zane thought furiously at his brother, 'I told you the boy is dead. I don't do dead bodies!'

Lucas shrugged at him and Zane knew he'd heard. Lucas's range wasn't great, but at this distance, he could read anything Zane thought if Zane put a little force behind it. 'We're just going to disappoint her,' Zane added.

"We know you need closure, Diane," Lucas continued, and although ostensibly his words were directed to the mother, his eyes were on Zane's.

"I know there's not much hope." Diane's words were soft. "But not knowing? Never knowing? It'll kill me. I would never have thought I'd turn to a psychic for help, but I'm desperate."

Zane tried not to sigh, to smile reassuringly. "You know there are a lot of fake psychics in the world, right?"

"I'm desperate," she repeated. "Anything you can do."

Great. She was going to turn into one of those people who poured their life savings into charlatans if he didn't find something, he just knew it.

He glared at Lucas again. 'You owe me for this.' Lucas nodded and he knew he'd gotten his message across, as he took Diane's hand and tried to focus on finding.

❧

"I can't really push you, sweetie."

"Wanna go high," demanded the little boy, his lower lip pouting.

Akira sighed and looked back at the house. She hoped no one was looking. Grabbing the metal chains that held the swing, she pulled it back, up and up, as high as she could reach, and then let it go. He chortled with delight as the swing fell and rose, fell and rose again.

"Again, again," he begged, and Akira obeyed, a reluctant smile curving her lips.

"Is this where you died, honey?" she asked, trying to make the question casual. She didn't want to upset him again. The storm of ghost tears that she'd precipitated the first time she'd asked still stained his face.

"Mama said no," he answered sadly. "No swing, too little." At the highest height of the swing, with a squeal of glee, he pushed himself off, and fell, tumbling through the air. Akira couldn't resist the gasp of horror and the instinctive grab, but it was hopeless. Even if he'd been flesh-and-blood, she couldn't have caught him. For a moment, a bare second, he was a crumpled shadow on the ground, and then he bounced back up again.

This was where he'd died, she realized. And it wasn't a murder-suicide but an accident-suicide.

"Can you help him?"

At the sound of the voice behind her, Akira whirled. It was the ghost from the house, edges still quivering and flashing. She took two steps backward.

"No, please," said the ghost, reaching out a hand to her, but not moving forward. "I know you can see him. See us. I don't mean to scare you. But please help him."

Akira swallowed. "Help him how?" she asked, trying to keep her voice steady.

"I can't get close to him," the ghost told her. "Something starts to happen when I do. I think it hurts him?"

Akira nodded. This she knew. "Your energy is too strong. You suck in power from your surroundings and when you get near another ghost, you—well, rip him apart, basically." She took another step backward, not feeling inclined to mention what he could do to her.

"But why?" he asked, voice despairing, energy level flickering a little higher. "I didn't start this way."

Oh, dear. Should she try to run? "Despair, grief, anger," she answered. "The more upset you get, the more energy you pull in. At a certain point, it works like an overdose of neurotransmitters might in a living human."

"Which means what?"

Akira took a deep breath. Should she be telling him this? Was she going to make it worse? But something about his looks—the lanky build, the shaggy hair, the deep brown eyes, the wire-rimmed glasses, the pale skin—said intellectual to her. "There's a theory that psychosis is caused by excess dopamine. The energy does something like that."

"I'm going to lose my mind?" He sounded horrified.

"If you don't calm down, um, yes."

"How can I calm down?" His energy jumped a little higher, the pink deepening. "I'm a ghost!"

Akira's heart was starting to pound in her ears. She took another step away, glancing behind her to check for obstacles. "If you don't, you'll destroy your son," she pointed out, hoping that she was right about the accident. If he had murdered his son once, a second time might not seem like an obstacle.

"Dada?" The little ghost boy wandered forward, and his father hastily shifted away. The boy plopped down on the ground, and started to weep. Akira crouched next to him, wanting to console him, not sure how.

"Calm, calm," the father repeated. Akira could see him taking deep breaths and for a moment, she wondered what breathing felt like when you were a ghost. But his red edges pulled back a little, the aura around him diminishing. "Can you help him?"

What was he asking her to do? Akira wondered. Set up a ghost orphanage? She imagined, briefly, bringing the swing set back to Florida and putting it up in her back yard. The little ghost boy could join the bigger boys. Maybe they'd have fun together. But then she tried to envision explaining to the tearful woman inside why she wanted the swing set and shook her head. That was never going to work. "What do you want me to do?" she asked.

"I never expected this to happen," the father said. "I thought dead was dead. The heart stops beating, the brain shuts off, life is over."

Akira eyed him warily. He didn't seem upset about the discovery, not really. Not like the religious ghost she'd met once who was very, very angry about not being in heaven. Akira stretched her hand, opening and closing the fingers. Sometimes those bones still ached.

"But this can't happen to everyone. I've looked for others. I went to the cemetery, the hospital."

"Hospitals usually have a few spirits hanging around." Akira was trying to be cautious, watching the light around the ghost for any hint that he was losing control. But he seemed to be calming and he was being careful, too, staying several feet away from her and the little boy.

"Yes," he agreed. "But one disappeared while I was talking to him. And another asked me if I saw a door, and then faded away. So there has to be somewhere else, not just here. And some way to get there."

Akira frowned. A door? She'd interacted with a lot of ghosts and they did disappear. When she was young, she thought they went somewhere, but her father had scoffed at that. They were just energy, he insisted, energy changing forms. "How did you talk to them?" she asked. The flaring around his edges would be dangerous for any other ghosts in his vicinity: how had he gotten close enough?

"This didn't start until I found Daniel and realized what I'd done," the ghost answered her, a look of pain crossing his face as he looked down at the boy, still sitting on the ground. Akira nodded. That was why she avoided certain subjects with ghosts. Even seemingly calm spirits could get dangerous if they got too upset.

"And I've been trying so hard to get someone inside to listen to me, but they just won't."

Akira stood. The boy was no longer weeping, just playing with the grass, trying to make blades move to no avail. "They can't see you or hear you."

"Yes," he agreed. "Why can you?"

Akira lifted one shoulder in a shrug. "Just lucky, I guess." She tried to keep the words light.

"Not so lucky if you're scared of me," the ghost answered. "I won't hurt you. Not on purpose, anyway."

Hmm, Akira thought. He was perceptive for a ghost. Or maybe a hint of her true feelings had slipped out. But she could see that his edges had started to solidify. He was calming down.

"I thought maybe we were trapped here until there was a service. You know, a funeral. But they'll never find our bodies."

Akira knew that wasn't right. She was quite sure that Dillon had had a proper funeral, as had plenty of the ghosts she'd known in the past. A funeral wasn't a magic ticket to another world. But she glanced at the house, thinking of the woman inside. She didn't want to lie to this ghost, but maybe she didn't need to tell him the whole truth, either.

"Do you want me to tell them where your bodies are?" she asked, trying to keep her voice neutral.

~

A relative. Damn it. She was about to talk to a relative.

These things just never ended well.

Akira stood in the doorway, trying to decide what to say, how to approach the subject. Oh, by the way, your ex-husband was just careless, not malicious? He didn't actually murder your kid, just hid the body? No, that wasn't the right starting place.

Zane and the blonde woman were sitting on the couch, Zane holding both of the woman's hands in his. Although she knew there was nothing romantic or sexual in the touch, Akira felt a slight prickle of annoyance. Not that there was anything serious between her and Zane, but still, somewhere less than twelve hours ago, those hands had been touching her in very intimate places. Seeing them touching another woman just felt wrong.

Lucas was standing next to Zane, watching his brother. Two men stood a few steps behind him, also watching intently. FBI agents, Akira wondered? They could be, she supposed. They fit her stereotypical image of FBI agents, with unflattering suits, boring ties, and short hair. Farther away, where the family room met the kitchen, another cluster of people stood gathered around a table, some with heads down over a map, some talking in quiet voices.

So many people, she thought. Hell. Could she really do this? Before she had a chance to decide, a shock—as if she'd just been doused with ice water—ran through her. She shuddered convulsively and gasped, feeling the energy pouring into her veins, jolting its way along her spine. The adult ghost appeared inside the room, no longer pink-tinged.

"Don't do that," she hissed at him. Ugh, it hurt. She shivered again, blinking back tears of pain.

"You could feel me?" he asked, surprised, as the people closest to the door, including Zane, all looked in Akira's direction.

"Of course I can," she started to say irritably, but before more than the second word slipped through her lips, she noticed the people looking at her and pressed her lips together, looking up and away and at anything but them.

Before she had time to do more than take another breath, Zane was standing in front of her, his hands on her shoulders. "You okay?" he asked. She looked up at him. His face was serious and she could see the worry in his eyes.

She had told him nothing about ghosts, she realized. Nothing at all. All he knew was that she didn't want people to know she could see them, and that she didn't like having her ability. And yet he was still worried about her, still quick to jump up from what he was doing to make sure that nothing was wrong. She nodded at him and tried to smile.

"They're both ghosts," she whispered to him. "And both here."

His eyes widened just slightly and he glanced over his shoulder at the woman sitting on the couch and then quickly back at Akira. "What do you want to do?" he asked her in a hushed voice.

She shrugged uncertainly, feeling helpless. "Did you tell Lucas? About Dillon?" Grace and Nat and Max and Zane had all spent some time sitting in the car after Akira had confirmed that it was, in fact, haunted and that Dillon could hear them, but only Zane regularly visited. Akira didn't know whether that was because Zane had warned the others off or whether it was too painful for them. The idea of a ghost could be comforting, but it was also an ever-present reminder of loss. She understood if it was easiest for the Latimers to let Dillon be, trusting that he was okay in her company.

She paused, because Zane was shaking his head no. "We decided to wait until he was home for a visit."

"So, does he know about me?" she whispered. "My, um, quirk, I mean?"

Zane shook his head no again. But he didn't have a chance to say anything further, because Lucas was abruptly speaking, his voice carrying across the room, "Folks, we need some privacy for a while. Please clear the room. Jane, why don't you set up in the front? Mark, maybe you could take a couple of people on a lunch run?" Quickly, efficiently, almost ruthlessly, and within the space of sixty seconds, everyone except Lucas, Diane, Zane, Akira—and the ghost—was out of earshot.

"He really does read minds, doesn't he?" Akira said to Zane.

He managed a smile. "How'd you guess?"

"All right, what was that about Dillon?" Lucas asked, crossing to where they were standing.

"Dillon?" Diane stood, also joining them by the door. "What's going on? Who's Dillon? Is there someone out there?"

Akira looked at them, at Lucas' frown, Diane's worry, Zane's concern for her.

Great.

Double the relatives, double the trouble. Then she took a deep breath and started to explain.

Diane fainted. Then she cried. Then she got mad. Akira was impressed with the range of her vocabulary and secretly glad that her ex-husband was the ghost and not Diane. She didn't want to know what Diane's energy would look like, and Rob took the yelling without as much as a flicker of his own energy. Then Diane cried again.

Lucas, though, got colder. The charm disappeared, leaving only the dangerous toughness in its place. If he'd been the brother interviewing her in Tassamara, Akira would never have taken the job, she knew. And while Diane cried and screamed, he disappeared to arrange the search for the bodies.

Rob had lost his job several months ago, he told Akira. The house was headed into foreclosure, and he and Diane had split up. He'd bought the swing set when Diane was pregnant, and Diane had always said it was too big for the boy. When Daniel fell while Rob was at the house taking care of him, Rob broke. He'd taken Daniel's body and driven the car to an old quarry that was filled with water, a place that he and Diane had gone diving in earlier, happier days. He'd headed straight into the water. He hadn't been thinking about a next, about what happened after, he'd just despaired.

"I couldn't imagine telling her," Rob said, watching Diane cry. "I didn't know how much worse it would be not to be able to tell her."

She nodded. He wasn't the first ghost she'd met who had been surprised and frustrated by his afterlife.

"So what happens now?" he asked.

Akira shrugged. Personally, she was hoping for a ride back to the airport and a smooth flight home. But he wouldn't mean what would happen to her, he wanted to know what would happen to him and Daniel and she had no idea.

"Aren't you supposed to find us a white light?"

Akira sighed. She'd warmed up to Rob's ghost during the past half-hour and if he could handle Diane's diatribes without losing control, he could probably handle what she had to say, too. "The 1970's has a lot to answer for. Watergate, bellbottoms, disco. And that whole white light idea."

Zane was perched on the couch next to the sobbing Diane, patting her back helplessly and handing her tissues. At Akira's words, he looked up. She could read the plea in his eyes, and she tucked her hands behind her back and sidled sideways, closer to the door. He was doing a fine job with the tissues, much better than she would in his place. His look changed to one of mild exasperation and she tried to look apologetic without implying that she would be helpful. Crying relatives were better than angry relatives but not by much. She never knew what to say or do.

"I suppose that makes sense," Rob said. "In the earliest afterlife myths, there's no white light. In fact, in Plato's Republic, in the story of Er, there's a rainbow."

"The story of who?" Akira asked.

"Er. Yes, Er. Not Um. I know the jokes." He was looking around. "But there should be a passageway first. A door. A staircase. Something like that."

Abruptly, he disappeared. Startled, Akira looked around. Was he gone? But no, he'd just walked through the glass. He was outside, talking to the little boy. Now that Akira had absorbed some of his energy and he had calmed down, he could get close to the little ghost without hurting him. Akira slid open the door and stepped out onto the patio.

"Do you see a door, Daniel?" the father was saying.

"Dada, Dada," the little boy chortled happily, hugging his father's legs. "Dada."

"Oh, Daniel," Rob scooped the ghost boy up, hugging him close, and burying his face in the boy's blond head for a second. Then he said again, "Do you see a door, Daniel? Look around really carefully."

The boy obeyed, then shook his head. "Back door, Dada?" he asked, pointing at the house.

"Not the door to the house, another door."

Daniel shook his head again, then frowned, and kicked to be let down. "Dis way?" He sounded almost curious, as he walked past the swing set. Rob watched him, eyes searching as if he was trying to see what Daniel was seeing. "Come, Dada," the boy ordered, holding out his hand. "Come wit me."

"I don't see it, Daniel." Rob sounded sad. "But you go ahead."

"No, Dada." The little boy shook his head, and waved at his father imperiously. "You come. Come me. Dis way. You see?"

The grief on Rob's face was so intense that Akira could hardly bear to look at him, and his voice was choked, as he repeated, "I don't see it, Daniel. You go ahead and I'll—and I'll catch up to you someday."

"No, Dada." Returning to his father's side, Daniel took Rob's hand. "Dis way," he insisted.

Rob looked down and smiled sadly, letting himself be tugged along, as he said, "I'll come with you as far as I can, Daniel, but then you have to go on your own, all right? You won't know her but Grandma will be waiting for you and you'll like . . . oh."

On that final word—a startled but at the same time almost calm exclamation—Rob and Daniel disappeared.

☙CHAPTER ELEVEN❧

Ghosts disappeared.

They'd be there one day, and then the next, they weren't. Nothing about that surprised Akira.

But they didn't disappear because they went somewhere.

Where was there to go? They disappeared because they were energy, and the energy changed forms or dissipated, right?

Right?

Akira sighed. She was staring out the window of the plane, waiting for everyone else to take their seats, and trying to think through what had happened today. Oh, not the drama of it all. Not the emotions, the people, the dynamics, the complicated stuff. She just wanted to understand the science.

Damn it, ghosts were energy. They didn't go places. Of course, theoretically, other dimensions could exist. The cosmological multiverse theories postulated a potentially vast number of universes. In fact, there was a cosmologist—at MIT, maybe?—who was working on a taxonomy of universes beyond the observable one that people experienced every day. She wondered what he would have to say if she could tell him what she saw.

"You okay?" Zane was buckling himself into the seat next to her, pulling the long shoulder strap across his body and snapping it into the clasp, but his worried eyes were locked on her face.

She ignored his question. "I've wasted a decade of my life," she said, as the realization hit her.

He didn't smile, just tilted his head as if encouraging her to go on.

"Energy research. I should have been studying quantum physics all this time." She shook her head. She'd gone into physics to try to understand the way the universe worked, and she'd focused on energy because her father had always insisted that the ghosts she saw were just energy.

She frowned. Well, not always. In her earliest memories, it had been different. But from the time they'd settled in Santa Marita, he'd told her that what she saw was a form of energy.

Zane picked up her hand and she let him take it, watching as he laced their fingers together, still thinking about her father, until, dropping his voice, Zane asked her, "Do quantum physicists study resonant frequencies?"

She couldn't not smile at him. "Not really, no."

"Not wasted then," he murmured, leaning forward to take her lips. She opened to him, feeling his tongue trace its way into her mouth and a surge of desire sparking in her stomach and spreading warmth through her veins. God, it felt like days since he had touched her, but it was just hours since they'd woken up together. What a weird day it had been.

She pulled away, but let her hand slide up to cup his cheek. "Do you do that often?" She was thinking of the woman they'd left behind, currently lost in a fog of grief. The strength of Diane's anger had made Akira think that she was tough enough to be okay someday, but someday wasn't going to be soon. They'd left while the news media filled the street, FBI agents the house, but tomorrow, or maybe the next day, Diane would wake up to emptiness. Akira remembered what that felt like. And the loss of a child must be even worse: she hoped Diane had someone who could be there for her.

"Kiss you? Not often enough."

This time, her smile wasn't even reluctant. "No. I mean look for missing people."

Zane grimaced. "I prefer insurance cases."

"To finding kids?"

"Or not finding them."

"A good shrink could help you with that problem," Lucas drawled, snapping himself into the seat across from Akira.

Reluctantly, she pulled her gaze off Zane and looked at his older brother. She didn't like him. She might not be being fair, she acknowledged to herself: her perceptions were undoubtedly colored by the gauntlet of reporters she and Zane had had to push their way through to get into the house, and the fear she still had that her image was going to wind up on some evening news show as a helpful psychic. Diane had promised not to tell anyone what had happened, but who knew how trustworthy the distraught and bereaved mother was?

"I didn't know you were with him," Lucas said gently.

That didn't make it better. He was still taking advantage of his brother. Why should Zane have to follow Lucas's every whim?

"Dragging Diane out to the airport seemed cruel, especially when Zane didn't think he could help. Why give her false hope? Plus, every reporter and cameraman in North Carolina would have been right behind her."

Yeah, and then there was the mind-reading thing. It just seemed so rude.

"Well, then, don't think so loudly." A smile was playing around Lucas's lips. Akira glared at him.

"He doesn't usually do that," Zane interjected, squeezing the hand he was still holding. "Ignore him."

"Except for the part about the shrink," Lucas corrected him. "Your inability to find dead bodies is just a mental block. If you can find a diamond, you can find a dead body."

Akira frowned.

"Well, I can't," Zane said flatly.

But it didn't make sense that he couldn't. "If you can find a mineral that's measurably indistinguishable from another lump of the same mineral, then finding a specific mass of DNA, living or dead, shouldn't be hard," Akira said.

"It doesn't work that way." Zane shook his head. "If it was that simple, I wouldn't be able to find anything. Everything would all blend together."

"Not finding dead bodies is a defense mechanism." Lucas leaned back in his seat and closed his eyes, as if to say that the old argument was at an end, as the plane's engines roared to life.

A defense mechanism? Akira tried to imagine what Zane's life would be like if he could find dead bodies. How many people went missing every day? How many of them wound up dead? How many hours would he spend just like this, sitting in a plane, waiting to fly to or from a scene like the one they'd just left?

It wasn't that she was unsympathetic to Diane, but it seemed to her that Zane's gift was more like hers than she'd realized: once it was revealed, his life would no longer belong to him. It would be an endless stream of desperate people, tragic situations, grief and pain.

"Or a coping strategy," Akira suggested. Her words were almost drowned out by the noise of the engines as they accelerated down the runway, but Lucas opened his eyes and looked at her. She met his gaze evenly. Maybe she'd reserve judgment on Zane's brother. He was Dillon's father, after all.

Zane squeezed her hand again and she looked back at him, at his wry smile, the affection in his eyes. She should tell him about ghosts. She needed to tell him about ghosts, about their violent energy, about what they could do, both to her and to other ghosts. But if she did . . .

Maybe she should think about what she'd learned today a little more first. It didn't change the risk: angry ghosts weren't like people, it wasn't possible to have conversations with them. They were much too dangerous for that. But if ghosts actually went somewhere when they disappeared? She needed to consider what that meant, see how it might change her ideas about past events.

"Think we can make tomorrow a do-over on today?" Zane asked her, voice low, just for her ears. She raised her brows in question. "Start the day the same way, but stay in bed a whole lot longer? Then maybe brunch at Maggie's? She makes incredible waffles. And then I'll take you to the springs. We can kayak, maybe see an alligator? Go for a swim if you like really cold water?"

Okay, yeah, she was definitely not telling him about the ghosts. Possession, convulsions, broken bones, possible death—they were so decidedly unromantic. She'd have to tell him eventually, but the fun would be over then, and she really wanted just a little while to enjoy this—to enjoy him—first.

She smiled. "Sounds perfect."

❧

"Earth to Akira."

"Hmm?" Akira responded absently, not looking up from her phone. She was trying to organize her past experiences with ghosts into categories, but it was proving much more challenging than she'd expected.

She'd always thought that ghosts came in types. There were the faders, the confused, the free, the tied, and then the red-edged.

Except in hospitals, the faders were the most common. Sometimes she thought they were more like memories than conscious beings. Like the boys in the backyard, who did nothing but run and play and laugh, faders seemed to be living and reliving important moments, as if they were an afterimage of a life, not an extension of the life itself. Akira called them faders because they were usually translucent, but the amount of translucency varied. She suspected that the older the ghosts, the more translucent they were.

Then there were the confused. Most often, they seemed to be the recently dead. Hospitals were riddled with them, and they could far too easily start developing red edges. But they tended to disappear quickly. More than any other type of ghost, one minute they were there, and the next, they were gone.

"Akira," Zane's voice was more insistent and she shook her head, as if coming out of a dream, and turned to him.

"Yes?"

"The plane's landed. Lucas suggests we have dinner at the house?"

"House?" Akira was still distracted, still lost in her thoughts. That one time at the hospital, the time with the broken ribs. Had that ghost said something about a door? She had, hadn't she? What was it, exactly? She'd been nice for a ghost, worried about Akira. She'd asked if Akira wanted to come with her before she vanished. And she had mentioned a door. Okay, that meant at least one checkmark in the confused column.

"The house where I live?" Zane repeated patiently. "Lucas stays with us when he's in town. He'd like a chance to shower and change, and then have us meet him there. With Dillon?"

"Um, right, yes." Akira glanced down at her phone, tapping it to close the spreadsheet app she'd been using. Dillon. His dad. Dinner. Right. All of that made sense. Lucas was here to talk to Dillon and she was sure that Dillon would want to see him. She could do that.

But if ghosts could go through doors, why were the tied spirits stuck? Like Dillon. If a door was available to him, why would he have spent years sitting in a car hoping something interesting would happen?

"Akira." A gentle finger was turning her chin until she was looking directly at Zane. "You good to talk to Dillon and Lucas?"

Finally breaking out of her reverie, Akira smiled at Zane. "Yeah, I'm fine. Dinner at your house or whatever works is great. I'm sorry I'm so distracted. I'm still trying to figure out what happened today."

"A ghost told you where his dead body was?" Zane offered.

"Also new," Akira agreed as she unbuckled her seat belt and followed Zane out of the plane's door, hopping down to the ground.

"But no. It was the way he disappeared."

"That was weird?" Zane asked.

Akira shrugged. "Different, anyway."

As they got in the car, she took out her phone again. She was careful about asking ghosts questions. Maybe too careful. Had Mr. Sato, her neighbor, been tied or free? She'd never seen him outside his yard, but she didn't know whether he chose to be there or not. And after Mrs. Sato died, she'd never been back in the house. She assumed he'd disappeared, but she didn't really know for sure.

So many ghosts she'd seen only briefly. And her earliest memories were so confused. She barely remembered anything from before her mother died, and the few years after that—well, those memories were chaotic at best. She was trying to remember: that first time, the time with the broken arm, what had that ghost been like? But it was too long ago, the memories just wisps of vision and feeling. Her father had been yelling, trying to cast the demon out of her, and her mother crying, and then there was pain. If anything, the clearest part of that memory was the smell of the hospital, that almost acrid antiseptic flavor that hospital air so often had.

"Christians—some of them anyway—think ghosts are actually Satanic," Akira mused, not looking away from her phone. She felt, more than saw, Zane glance at her. They'd taken his car to the airport, so that Dillon could stay home with Rose and Henry, so they were on their way to get the Taurus before heading to his house. "I think it's in Deuteronomy that the Bible expressly forbids communicating with the dead. People who talk to the dead are abominations or detestable, something like that."

"In some Buddhist monasteries, the monks leave offerings for ghosts before meals. Food or money or flowers," Zane answered, stopping at the red light in town. They'd been silent through the drive, Akira lost in her memories, Zane not disturbing her concentration.

Akira looked up, startled by his response. "How do you know that?"

He looked her way again, and grinned. "What, you don't think I'm a closet Buddhist?"

She laughed. She knew some Buddhists in California, and it seemed unlikely. "Are you?"

"Nah." He shook his head. "But I've been doing some reading."

"About religion?" Akira asked, surprised again. That seemed even more unlikely than Zane being a burger-eating Buddhist.

He shot her a tolerant look and said, "About ghosts. Now that I know they're real, it seemed like a good idea to learn a little more about them."

Oh, of course. "Learn anything interesting?" Akira asked, curious. Years ago, she'd read ghost stories and traditions obsessively, trying to find anything that would help make her make sense of her world. But she'd given up: too many stories, too much conflicting information, and too little of it that fit with her experiences. Maybe nuggets of wisdom were buried in the myths, but most of them were from a time before modern science.

"Lots," he drawled. "Anything that's true? I've got no idea."

"Probably not much," she told him. "Although maybe I know less than I used to think I knew."

"How so?"

On the plane, Lucas and Zane had quickly settled in to talking about business, which had been fine with Akira. She hadn't really wanted to talk to Zane about ghosts. She wanted waffles. She wanted to go kayaking. She wanted to see her first real alligator in the wild. She—maybe—wanted to go swimming, if the day was warm enough and the water not too incredibly cold. What she did not want was to scare Zane off by seeming obsessed with death, a phrase that lingered in her memory like a bitter aftertaste from an otherwise utterly forgettable past lover.

Now she shook her head, looking down at her phone again. "The little boy today? He took his father somewhere. The father, Rob, was saying that he couldn't go and then they disappeared. Together. That has to mean something, but I have no idea what."

"Hmm, that's interesting," Zane answered. "Not a—?"

"Don't even go there," Akira interrupted him, as he pulled up in front of the house. "It was not a white light. Or at least Rob didn't see a white light. And Daniel . . ." She tried to remember his exact words but failed, and, mystified, added, "I don't know what he saw. He said something like, 'come this way,' and then they disappeared together."

"So you're thinking?"

Akira shook her head again. "Let me get Dillon," she said. "Would you mind driving?" She wanted to keep adding observations to her spreadsheet.

Ten minutes later, they were on the road again, and Akira and Dillon were having a friendly argument accompanied by Zane's interested silence.

"But maybe if you helped me resolve my lingering issues . . ."

"Psychobabble," Akira interrupted Dillon. "I've tried that, really I have. And it doesn't work. Unless ghosts are completely oblivious to their real issues and the ones I've tried to help were sending me off on wild goose chases."

"Okay, I'm not asking for a white light, but a door would be awesome." Dillon was leaning forward from his usual spot in the middle of the backseat, cheeks flushed with ghostly excitement.

"Dude, you've talked to your relatives. What exactly do you think you could say that would make a difference?" Akira wished she hadn't given Dillon this glimpse of hope.

"Maybe I need to talk to my Dad?" Dillon offered. "Or, you know, let my Dad talk to me? He's probably pretty pissed off."

Akira sighed. "There was this one ghost. When I was in college?" she told him. "I returned her library books. I transcribed a paper for a class on English romantic poets for her. Seriously, I did everything she could think of that she hadn't finished. It wasn't fun. And nothing worked. It didn't make a difference. She was still haunting the café down the street from the library when I graduated."

Dillon flopped back with a sigh.

"No ghostly roads, huh?" Zane asked, turning onto a narrow road.

"A road?" Akira asked, looking at him. Where had he come up with that idea? Daniel hadn't said anything about a road, but then he'd been very vague.

"Native American tradition," Zane replied. "Ghosts stick around for a year, then take the ghost road in the sky. Maybe Dillon needs to look up at night?"

"Ha," Dillon replied from the backseat. "He forgets how much time I've spent in a parking lot. Not much to look at except the sky. No, I'd know if there was a road. It's okay, Akira. My life—well, or whatever you want to call it—is good these days. I don't need a door or a road."

Akira looked over her shoulder, and smiled to acknowledge what he'd said, then glanced at Zane as he pulled the car to a halt. "No roads in the sky either."

Zane grinned at her. "I'll keep reading."

"You do that." Akira unbuckled her seat belt and turned, reaching for the door, a smile tugging at her lips. Maybe in a different mood, at a different time, she would have been worried that he was researching ghosts, anxious about what he might be thinking, but right now, today? Today, it felt sweet.

And then she stopped, hand on the door, smile gone as if it had never been.

The house.

Oh, shit.

The house.

She'd been half expecting it to be ostentatious, but it wasn't: a big white farmhouse, it was two stories with shutters on the windows and a wide porch extending half the length and then bending around the side, and lovely landscaping, with plenty of the bright flowers that made Florida so colorful.

It should have been beautiful.

And it would have been, if it hadn't been so very, very haunted.

The house in North Carolina had shimmered with energy; this house roiled with it, a crackling, snapping power as if it was trapped amidst a storm cloud that only she could see.

Fear surged within her. She felt her heart racing, her throat closing, a fuzzy feeling in her legs that let her know her knees wouldn't hold her . . . and then it doubled, trebled.

"Dillon," she gasped, but the name was nothing but a puff of air he could never have heard, even if he wasn't already out of the car, strolling toward the porch, unconcerned about the deadly vortex that would rip him apart when he got too close.

"Dillon," she tried again, louder this time, but he was too far away, farther every second, and the door was closed. She looked at him, looked at the house, and then she turned to Zane.

"Drive," she ordered. "Drive!"

⁓CHAPTER TWELVE⁓

Zane recognized the tone.

He moved without hesitation, sliding back into the seat that he'd been half out of, smoothly restarting the car, backing, turning, accelerating away, all without a single pause or wasted movement. Akira, still in the passenger seat, had her eyes closed, her clenched fists held to her mouth.

Was she in pain? He couldn't tell but he didn't ask questions.

He just drove.

Once, with Lucas, he'd heard the same order, delivered in the same voice. It was a routine job, or as routine as any job with Lucas ever was. They'd been in the Pacific Northwest, helping out on a DEA case. Zane had pinpointed the location of a stash of drugs using a low-level drug dealer as his link, and Lucas had gone in to take a look around. Returning to the car, he'd snapped out his orders. Zane didn't notice the blood seeping down Lucas's arm until they were a mile down the road and Lucas had called in reinforcements.

Now he glanced at Akira. Her lips were moving, but he couldn't hear the words. "Do you need a hospital?" he asked, trying to calculate distances and times. He could call Nat, get her to meet them at the nearest emergency clinic.

"No," Akira snapped. She half-turned in her seat, craning her neck to look behind them, then turned even farther, lifting one knee onto the seat so that she was almost fully shifted. "Oh, God, Dillon," she murmured. "Why did I make you practice stretching?" And then she grimaced as if in agony, clapped her hands against her ears, and fell back into her seat.

"I'm sorry, I'm sorry," she babbled. "I'm sorry."

"Akira, what the hell is going on? What do you need?" Zane asked, a little desperately. She was acting crazy, but something was happening that he couldn't see, he was sure of it. But not seeing left him feeling helpless. What could he do?

She shook her head. "Are you okay?" She was talking to the

backseat.

Zane couldn't help being a little annoyed. He didn't like feeling helpless, he didn't like not knowing what was happening, and he didn't like that she was talking to his nephew and not to him.

"I'm sorry," she said again, "But that house is haunted!"

All right, maybe she had gone crazy. Her house was haunted, her car was haunted, her whole damn life was haunted. What was her problem with one more ghost? But chalk up another point for Max's serendipity. He'd been saying the house was haunted for years, since right after Dillon and Mom died.

"You don't understand," Akira said.

"That makes two of us," Zane muttered, turning off the narrow road that led to the house, and onto the busier road that led back to town. He wasn't sure where he was going, but he'd head back to Akira's house for the moment.

He felt more than saw her glance at him, so he looked in her direction. She was looking pale again, dark smudges under her eyes. He felt a pang of concern. Tired was okay—they hadn't gotten a lot of sleep the night before—but she looked more anxious than he'd seen her in weeks.

She was so not his type, he thought. He liked easy. Not sexually (although he didn't object to that) but emotionally. Uncomplicated. Cheerful. Go to a few movies, out to dinner, hang out with friends, maybe spend some time outside at the beach or the springs. And in a few months, when they were both a little bored, move on as friends. This business of worrying about whether a woman was hurting was just not his style.

"Talk," he ordered. "And put on your seat belt."

She smiled faintly, and buckling up, said, "I warned you. The very first time we met. I told you to stay away from the ghosts that are all red around their edges." That must be directed to Dillon, Zane realized. She'd definitely never told him anything about red ghosts. Really, they'd barely talked about ghosts at all.

"There is! Inside!" she insisted. "You're just lucky you didn't get past the door."

Zane's phone started vibrating and he glanced at it. Lucas, he'd guess. Wondering what had just happened. If Zane knew, he'd answer the call, but since he didn't, he ignored his phone, and kept listening to Akira's one-sided conversation.

"Well, stopping because your dad came outside saved you then. If you'd gone inside, the energy would have ripped you apart. It's like being caught in a whirlpool or a tornado."

A tornado? He'd read about something like that, hadn't he? Zane tried to remember what he'd seen about ghostly tornadoes.

"Yes, of course, I know what I'm talking about. I've seen it happen." Akira's voice was almost angry, as if Dillon was arguing with her.

Vortexes, that's what he was remembering. Some ghost hunter site had said that it was one of the common types of ghostly experiences. But there was nothing about them being dangerous.

"Okay, fine, red like an aura, yes. No, not like an evil halo. Dillon, could you focus? This is serious."

Zane's lips quirked. He was almost able to imagine what Dillon was saying from Akira's responses. His nephew had always been curious, sometimes too curious for his own good. But the inadvertent memory of Dillon's experimentation lit a spark of sadness, and Zane sobered, as Akira continued, "Dangerous, dangerous. How many kinds of dangerous are there? It's a ghost that will rip you to pieces if you get close."

Okay, that didn't sound good. But it also didn't make any sense. "If there's a ghost in the house, it's my mom," Zane interrupted. "She would never hurt Dillon."

He glanced at Akira. She was chewing on her lower lip again, the way she did when she got nervous. "It's not—I don't think I'd call it your mom."

"I've lived in that house most of my life. It was definitely not haunted before my mom died."

"Maybe it started as your mom, but red ghosts, they're not conscious. They're not like people. They're not aware of what they're doing. They're just dangerous energy."

"But why?" Zane asked. "If it started as my mom's spirit . . ."

"Anger, sometimes," Akira answered him. "Angry ghosts lose control. Ghosts that want revenge go red, I think. Or, um . . ." she glanced at the backseat. "Despair, grief."

"That medium said—huh." Zane paused, remembering what had happened to the medium. He frowned, thinking back.

"Right. That medium." Akira was no longer chewing on her lip. Her chin had firmed and if he had to label her expression, he would have called it a glare. "Let's talk about her for a minute. So some medium shows up, tells you there are ghosts in your house, and then just goes away again?"

"Not exactly," he said.

She started to nod. "I knew it. I knew it. It's the only way a ghost gets that powerful. Damn it, you took me to a house with a killer ghost in it. You took us to a house with a killer ghost! Don't you realize what could have happened?"

"That medium died of natural causes," Zane answered her, hands tightening on the steering wheel. It had been strange, that was true. But still, Akira was saying that his mother—his mother, of all people—was a murderous ghost. No way. That just wasn't possible. "They did an autopsy. It was an aneurysm."

"Of course it was. Because medical examiners are so eager to write 'murder by spirit energy' on a death certificate," Akira snapped.

&

"I'll call you."

Damn it, Akira thought as she watched Zane's car pull away. She hated that phrase. Not just the words, but everything they encompassed. Both the sub-textual, "Yeah, you're a little too weird for me," and the implied, "And don't call me."

Not to mention the passive-aggressive dishonesty of the lie. He wouldn't call. She'd see him at work next week, and they'd both pretend that Friday night had never happened.

With a sigh, she picked up a box that was resting by the front door, then turned and sat down on the porch steps. The early evening was still warm, the air soft and fragrant. The orange blossoms that Meredith had promised had flowered weeks ago, but a vine twining its way around the porch had developed little white flowers. Akira was almost sure it was a weed, but the smell reminded her of jasmine and she liked it.

She was hungry. It had been a long day. She ought to go inside and make herself some dinner. But the thought of a solitary meal, probably pulled out of the freezer, nuked for five minutes in the microwave, and then eaten in front of her computer just wasn't appealing.

"You really think my grandma is a crazy ghost?" Dillon asked, hiking himself onto the railing next to her.

"I don't believe in theorizing ahead of the data," Akira answered gloomily. "It's bad science. But we can't exactly ask for introductions, so yeah, my best guess is that your grandma is a ghost."

"Another ghost?" Rose asked, appearing on the porch behind them. Akira barely jumped. "We should invite her over."

"Not this one," Akira sighed. As Dillon told Rose the story, she reflected on their ride home. Zane didn't want to believe that his mom was a malevolent ghost. Fair enough. She couldn't blame him for that. But he hadn't been happy to learn that ghosts could be dangerous, either. He hadn't been rude about it, but his silence was decidedly stubborn.

"That's too bad." With a careful flounce of her full skirts, Rose sat down next to Akira. With a perceptive sideways glance, she added, "That's not why you're sad, though. Where'd the dreamboat go?"

"He'll be back," Dillon said. "He just needs to talk to my family."

Akira pressed her lips together. She didn't want to tell Dillon he was wrong, but she didn't think so.

"Men," Rose's voice filled with disgust. "Rats, every one of them. Except Henry, of course."

"Hey," Dillon protested. "What about me?"

Rose waved a dismissive hand in his direction. "You would have turned into a rat, too. You wouldn't have been able to help yourself. I know your kind."

Akira felt the corners of her mouth pulling up in an involuntary smile. Had she thought her meal would be solitary? She'd been forgetting the crowd that lived at this house. Rose would be happy to talk her ear off while she ate, with Henry and Dillon providing an alternately encouraging and protesting chorus.

"What kind is that?" Akira asked. A neighbor, passing by on the street, glanced at her, face curious. Akira nodded, bringing her hand up to her ear to tap her headset. Oh, hell. She wasn't wearing it. She forced a smile, and the woman smiled back and walked on.

Right.

Tassamara.

The only small town in America where talking to yourself just made the neighbors think you were one of them.

"Men! They're all just out for one thing and once they've got it . . ." Rose snapped her fingers scornfully. "Except for Henry," she added again.

"Why except for Henry?" Akira began picking at the tape on the box. It was from Amazon, but she couldn't remember ordering anything.

"Henry was a wonderful boyfriend," Rose answered. "So sweet, so polite. Always a gentleman. My parents didn't approve, of course, but that wasn't Henry's fault. And he had nothing to do with—" Rose paused, and shrugged one shoulder, "—with what happened later."

Akira's brows went up, her eyes widening, her mouth dropping open. Henry? Rose and Henry had been boyfriend and girlfriend?

"You and Henry?" Dillon was almost spluttering with shock. "But—but—"

Akira pulled her mouth closed and waited, wondering what Dillon was going to say. The age difference didn't matter, of course: she could tell from the clothes that Henry had died much later than Rose had. But in the 1950's? In the segregated south? Henry had probably been risking his life to date a white girl.

"But he's old!" Dillon finally burst out. Akira smiled and continued working on the tape. Good for Dillon.

"He wasn't then, of course," Rose said impatiently. "That happened later."

"So did Henry live in the house, too?" Akira was curious. She'd assumed that all of the ghostly residents—the boys in the backyard, Rose, and Henry—had lived in the house at different times. It was unusual to find such a concentration of ghosts in one place, but not unthinkable.

"No." Rose looked puzzled for a minute and then thoughtful. "No, he only came to live here later. After, I mean. He never lived here when he was alive."

Huh. That was strange, Akira thought. What was Henry's tie to the house if he hadn't died here?

"It must have been nice for you when he got here," Dillon suggested. He'd obviously quickly recovered from the surprise. "You must have been lonely all by yourself."

"Oh, I wasn't by myself." Rose waved that idea off. "The boys were so much more fun back then. We had such a good time right after. We used to pester my little sister like you wouldn't believe." Rose giggled.

That was even more interesting. Akira wasn't surprised to find out that the boys in the backyard had been at the house longer than Rose. She was no expert on boys' clothing, but the slightly formal cut to their shorts, the collars on the button-down shirts, and even their socks made her think that they came from an older era, maybe around the 1920s. But she'd never really talked to them. If they were more active when Rose became a ghost, though . . .

With a last quick tug, she finally managed to get the tape off the box. Rose broke off the story of tormenting her sister that she'd been telling Dillon to say, "Ooh, what did you get?"

Akira folded back the cardboard sides of the box. She recognized the packaging on the object inside before even glancing at the packing slip.

It was a new Kindle.

She bit her lip. With a hand that felt suddenly cold, she picked up the paperwork. She was wrong.

It was two Kindles.

The note read, "One for you, one for Dillon. Grace says to tell him that if he intends to keep destroying them, she'll make it an official research project and buy them in bulk, but that he should leave yours alone. (Grace takes her reading seriously.)"

Damn it.

Akira blinked furiously. She would not cry. She would not cry. She would not cry.

But a tear overflowed anyway.

She'd really liked him.

❧

The phone rang.

Akira eyed it suspiciously.

She'd had a dream last night. At least she thought it was a dream, but the details were fuzzy. Still the uncertainty was at least half of why she was awake at this ridiculous hour. Ridiculous for a Sunday morning, anyway: it was barely after eight, and she'd just stepped out of the shower.

The phone rang again.

It was really too early for anyone to call. And her friends—the ones who would call her on a Sunday morning, anyway—were all in

California. They'd call at noon eastern time, not eight.

The phone rang a third time. If she didn't catch it before it rang again, it would go into voice mail. Akira lunged across the bed and grabbed the receiver. Sprawled in her messy blankets, she looked at the caller ID. Local, but she didn't recognize the number.

She pressed the button. "Hello?" She didn't deliberately play with the sound of her voice, but she also didn't try too hard to make it not sound husky with sleep. She had just gotten up after all.

"Waffles?"

It was a rush. Like the moment at the top of the roller coaster, right before the car tips over the edge of the hill. "You called me last night, didn't you?"

"I did. You were asleep."

"Mostly asleep," Akira corrected Zane.

"Mm-hmm." His voice was just as husky as hers. "You're a tease when you're sleepy."

"It was late," Akira defended herself, as she squeezed her eyes closed, trying to remember what she'd said. She could feel her cheeks turning pink, a flush half delight, half embarrassment.

He'd called.

"Yeah, I'm sorry about that." Zane sounded resigned. "The family discussions went on for a while. Too long. And—I hate to say it—they're crashing our breakfast, too."

"Oh." Akira knew her voice had flattened but she wasn't sure how she felt about that.

"Kayaking, after," he said hastily. "And then swimming? And dinner? And then back to your place and you can keep the promises you were making last night?"

A reluctant smile curved Akira's lips. She didn't remember any promises. But she'd like to keep them anyway. And hell, an hour of conversation about ghosts? She could do that.

❧

An hour later, she wasn't so sure.

She was seated at a table at the bistro with the entire Latimer family. Zane and Natalya were on either side of her, and Max, Grace, and Lucas were across the table. Despite the waffles, she felt a little like a criminal being interrogated by a panel of judges.

And she now understood exactly why Grace was CEO of General Directions. If their mom had been half as persistent as Grace was, it was no wonder she wasn't going quietly.

"I don't know," she answered for the umpteenth time, trying to hang on to her fraying patience.

"What about this one?" Grace asked, turning a book to show her a picture. Akira glanced at it. It was a black-and-white print in a style that looked distinctively Japanese to her.

"Were you cheating on your wife?" Akira asked Max. It was a rude question, but she didn't bother to cushion it.

"No, never," he answered readily and without hesitation.

"Then I don't think your mom has turned into an onryô," Akira told Grace.

Grace flipped the book back. "It says here that these ghosts can be created from grief and despair as well as a desire for revenge. Mom was definitely upset when she died."

"Every culture has traditions about ghosts. That doesn't mean that any of the stories are true." A passing waitress glanced at her and Akira smiled tightly. How had she gotten pulled into this conversation in a public place?

"Once you've accepted the impossible, questioning the improbable is only sensible." Max answered while Grace skimmed down the page, one finger trailing along the lines of text.

"Hmmm. To get rid of one of these ghosts, you're supposed to help it fulfill its purpose. That sounds familiar." Grace set the book down next to her plate on top of two others and reached for her tablet. Her waffles, like Akira's, were barely touched.

Zane nudged Akira with his elbow. She glanced at him, and he gestured at her plate with his head. "Eat," he said softly. "The sooner you finish, the sooner we can escape."

Akira raised an eyebrow, and then picked up her knife and fork. Lucas, Max and Grace seemed determined to learn everything they could about ghosts, while Zane and Natalya had been mostly quiet. But if Zane was offering escape . . .

"Not until we decide what to do," Grace said. "We need a plan, a strategic approach to the situation."

"What sort of a plan?" Natalya asked.

"This isn't another action item on your to-do list, Grace." Lucas shoved his plate away from him and gestured to the waitress for more coffee.

"I've been telling you for years that your mother was still here," Max said. "Maybe she just likes being with us."

Akira's mouth twisted. Sure, that might be true for some ghosts. But not the one that was haunting that house.

"If Mom's still here, there must be a reason for it," Grace protested. "Something she needs. Or wants. Right?" She looked at Akira questioningly.

Akira's eyes flickered to the waitress, and then she shrugged and sighed. Everyone in this town was crazy, anyway. Did it matter what they thought of her? "A ghost like the one in your house doesn't have consciousness," she answered. "Not like we think of it, anyway. There's no way to talk to it or communicate with it. If it was human, it'd be like, I don't know, like someone on a bad drug, hallucinating, psychotic, that kind of thing."

Lucas was frowning, Max was shaking his head, and Grace was reaching for another book.

"If Akira is right, Mom's ghost is dangerous," Lucas pointed out. His tone was grim. Of all of the Latimers, he was the one who seemed unhappiest.

"Either way, we need to help her move on. That's obvious." Grace was organized, determined, her mindset practical.

Natalya was quietly sitting back, either thoughtful or doubtful, Akira wasn't sure which, although maybe she felt both.

And Zane was the quietest of all. He'd greeted Akira, been friendly to the waitress, and then had been silent until he'd told Akira to eat. She had no idea what he was thinking. She glanced at him. He was watching her, eyes steady.

Hmm.

She recognized that look, and it had nothing to do with ghosts.

She took a careful bite of waffle, and chewed slowly, while she thought. Grace and Lucas were bickering—not with any malice, but with a friendly sibling obstinance—about what it might mean to have a ghost in their house.

There was no question in Akira's mind that the ghost was dangerous. None. Her usual approach would be to not get involved, to stay just as far away as possible. But yesterday's events had shown her that she didn't know everything that there was to know about ghosts. Not that she'd ever really thought she did, but she'd been comfortable with her own level of ignorance. But that door or passageway or whatever it was that the little boy had found—that was a mystery to her.

And it might be interesting to see what Grace, with all the resources of General Directions behind her, could learn about ghosts.

Akira took another bite of waffle, and delicately licked a drop of syrup off her lip. Her gaze flickered to Zane. Yes, he was watching her mouth. When he saw her looking at him, she smiled. That glow she felt? It also had nothing to do with ghosts.

"You've had enough, haven't you?" he asked.

She nodded, and put her silverware down.

"Thank God." It was half murmur, half groan, as he stood abruptly, reaching for her hand. She let him pull her to her feet, trying not to laugh.

"Wait," Grace ordered, putting up a hand to stop them.

"Nope," Zane answered, stepping away from the table. "Go hire some ghost busters or whatever. We've got plans."

"I don't know how to make a ghost go away," Akira told Grace, resisting Zane's tug on her hand. "I've never had any luck in getting even the ones I can communicate with to move on. But if I can answer your questions, I will."

"Tomorrow," Zane interrupted. "She'll answer your questions, tomorrow."

"Hang on." This time it was Lucas. "I still want—need—to talk to Dillon."

Zane paused. He sighed. He looked at Akira and she could see how badly he wanted to refuse.

She just smiled.

"Tell you what," she answered Lucas. "We'll hang out at my house for a while. Say, maybe until noon? I'll leave the car unlocked, and you can come to talk to Dillon, and before we go kayaking, I'll come tell you what he has to say." She looked back at Zane and kept her eyes steady on his, as she said to him, with all the innocence she could muster, "I'm sure we can think of something to do at my house for a couple of hours?"

~CHAPTER THIRTEEN~

Akira and Zane kayaked.

Eventually.

Akira didn't see an alligator on their first trip, but she did on their next, three weeks later.

Grace researched ghosts. Or rather Grace hired a researcher, who spent days poring over books of ghost stories and wrote concise reports of everything she'd learned for Grace at the end of every week. Grace brought the reports to Akira and they went over them line by line, Akira highlighting any kernels of information that fit with her experiences, crossing out those that didn't, and putting question marks by the ambiguous. The question marks always outnumbered the rest.

Akira and Zane played pool. And Halo. Also Skyrim, Mario Kart, Asteroids, Legend of Zelda, and even some Ms. Pac Man.

Grace hired a team of paranormal investigators to come investigate the house. They were thrilled with their energy readings, and excited about the EVP recordings they captured, but their suggestion to Grace that she firmly tell the ghost to leave was met with polite derision from Akira.

"Was your mom the kind of person who would have responded well to that?" she asked. "I mean even before she became a psychotic ghost?"

Zane snorted, Grace sighed.

Akira and Zane went to the beach. They splashed there, and swam at the springs, and floated in the pool in Akira's backyard, which was only three strokes across, even for Akira.

Grace interviewed mediums.

Of the three she found, two were actually sensitive enough to know when Dillon was around. Akira was impressed. Unfortunately, neither could communicate with him, even with the full trappings of a séance held in an office at GD headquarters.

"I've never really understood the séance thing," Akira mused from an adjoining office. There was no way she was opening herself up to ghostly possession, but she'd agreed to stay close enough that Dillon could attend and she could talk to him. "Why does lighting a few candles make a difference?"

"What am I supposed to do?" Dillon asked. "I don't see this spirit guide that's supposed to be talking to me. Do you?"

"Nope." Akira shrugged. "Maybe just try to knock on wood or something? Let me know when you're ready to quit," she added, as she opened up her Kindle. She'd just read a good book while she was waiting.

Akira and Zane went to Disneyworld. Akira screamed on Space Mountain, got wet on Splash Mountain, and shot more aliens than Zane on the Buzz Lightyear ride. They spent the night at the hotel that the monorail ran through the middle of, and watched the fireworks from the restaurant on top.

Grace searched for a priest willing to perform an exorcism. Apparently, though, the modern church required a bishop to grant permission to perform the rites of exorcism, and bishops preferred not to get involved with rumors of ghosts, especially non-Catholic ghosts. Akira was relieved: her memories were cloudy but she had a vague sense that exorcisms posed more risks than benefits.

As spring turned into summer, Akira got less enthusiastic about doing anything outside. She'd known Florida was going to be hot, but she hadn't expected Florida heat to be so very different from California heat.

"It's like living in a sauna," she said, watching the fan over her bed spin. It was so humid that she could almost see the blades of the fan slicing the thick air.

"You should let me get you a new air conditioner," Zane mumbled. "The one you have is crap." He was lying face down next to her.

"It's a rented house. The landlord is the one who has to buy a new air conditioner. Besides, I don't want an air conditioner."

He turned his head, opening his eyes lazily. "What do you want?"

Mischief glinted in Akira's eyes as she answered without looking at him, "Guess." She loved this game, mostly because he was so good at it. She was sure that quantum physics could explain his gift somehow, but it still felt almost magical when he used it on her.

He reached to touch her hand and she quickly pulled it away. "No touching," she said, laughing. "You have to get it without."

"Hmm." He squeezed his eyes closed and made a show of thinking hard. "Nope, no idea," he said, as he rolled over, tugging her until she was securely under him, his long legs tangled with hers, his hand stroking up her side.

She let herself be captured, lifting her lips to his, opening her mouth as he took her and tasted, lingering in a long, slow, languorous kiss, before pulling his head back and saying, tone almost startled, "Lemon Italian ice? From Jeremiah's? For breakfast?"

"Mmm," she murmured her agreement, eyelashes fluttering open. He felt so good, but it was so damn hot. "Wouldn't it taste amazing? Cold and tangy and perfect?"

"It would be good," he agreed, sitting up and looking around for his clothes.

"I didn't mean we had to go right now," Akira protested. What was his rush?

"We're not going." He grabbed his shorts. "I'm going. You're staying there. Right there. Exactly like that."

"Oh?" Akira smiled and stretched, loving the way his eyes followed her movement.

"The only thing better than lemon Italian ice on a too hot day," he murmured, leaning over her for one last hard kiss, "is lemon Italian ice in bed."

"It'll get all sticky," Akira objected, but not very seriously. She was already imagining his clever tongue cleaning up accidentally-on-purpose drips.

"Exactly."

Akira laughed as Zane grabbed his keys and wallet from the bedside table. He was so much fun. He had his moments of serious, of course—they'd had a few deep conversations late into the night, although there were certain subjects, like his ghostly mom, that they both avoided—but she'd never met anyone who enjoyed life like he did. Playing with him over these last few months had been amazing, the best time she'd ever had.

"Wait, take Dillon," she said as he turned to go. "He's been complaining that we're getting boring."

"Okay," he said agreeably, turning back and scooping up her keys from her dresser. "Back soon." As he headed out the door, she heard him calling, "Yo, Dillon. Mini road trip, bud."

Akira shook her head, still smiling. He was so accepting. It must have come from growing up in his family: if your older brother could read your mind and your older sister could tell your future, maybe you just became imperturbable from an early age. Zane talked to Dillon as if he was a physical presence, albeit one who couldn't talk back, and Dillon loved the company and conversation.

She turned onto her side and looked at the clock. Jeremiah's was over by the highway, at least twenty minutes away. And Zane might want her to wait right here, but she wasn't going to spend forty minutes in bed staring at the fan. She'd just do a quick load of laundry, she decided, and maybe make some iced tea.

With the washer running, she put the kettle on to boil, humming softly.

"Now there's a cheerful sound," Henry said from his seat at the table. "It's a fine day, isn't it?"

"It sure is," Akira agreed, turning to face him and leaning back against the counter while she waited for the water. She loved chatting with Henry. He was such a kindly presence, always pleasant, always warm.

But her smile faded as she looked at him, really looked at him. Was it the light? She glanced at the window, at the sunlight streaming in. She was usually at General Directions during the day, of course, and Zane was an annoyingly early riser: they were often out of the house by this time. But she'd never noticed the light making a difference to how she perceived other ghosts.

"Something wrong?" Henry asked, noticing her expression and looking concerned.

"No. No." Akira shook her head, and turned back to the tea. But her hands fumbled as she put the leaves into the strainer.

She could see through Henry. Not a lot, just a little. But he was definitely translucent.

And he'd never been translucent before.

Outside the kitchen window, she could see the boys, faint and almost transparent, running over the pool as if it didn't exist, playing in the heat as if it was spring instead of midsummer.

They were faders. Just memories of the people they'd once been.

She glanced over her shoulder. Henry had turned back to his newspaper, the ghostly paper that he read over and over again. And yes, she could definitely see beyond him to the wall on the other side of him.

That meant that Henry . . . Henry was a fader, too.

⁂

Tea made and poured over ice, Akira took the glass and slipped into the seat across from Henry.

She'd been thinking hard while her tea steeped. She hated questioning ghosts. It was impossible to know what might set them off, what careless phrase could change a peaceful encounter into a nightmare.

When her father had been alive, he'd been furious if he even caught her speaking to a ghost. As far as he was concerned, she was safest if she never even acknowledged that they existed, and he'd punished her harshly, trying to teach her that lesson. But living that way had proved impossible for Akira. And by now, she knew Henry. Or at least she thought she did.

"Anything interesting in the news?" she asked, voice casual.

"Oh, same old, same old," he answered, folding up his paper, and tucking it under his arm. "Hot enough for you today?"

Akira didn't answer. She was frowning into her glass, trying to decide how best to approach the subject. "Do you mind if I ask you some questions, Henry?" Maybe if she had his permission, he'd be less likely to get upset.

"Why, no. You go right ahead." He sounded surprised, and she understood why. They'd shared a table for months. Months in which they'd talked about the weather, the garden, the food she ate, her plans for the day, but never once anything personal.

"Do you remember how you died?"

"Of course." His answer was matter-of-fact. He leaned back in his chair, putting the folded newspaper on his lap. "It was cancer."

"Cancer? But—" Akira's eyebrows shot up in surprise.

"I'd had it for quite some time. Fought the good fight for a good few years. But in the end—eh, I think I just got tired. I was ready to let go."

Akira frowned. Most ghosts died quickly. Unexpectedly. Often violently. Akira didn't know whether she'd ever met one who'd anticipated his or her death before.

"I wasn't a young man. It wasn't a tragedy." Henry reached out a hand, as if to pat hers comfortingly, before pulling it back before it could sizzle its way through her skin.

Akira took a sip of her tea. She put the glass down, precisely on top of the ring of moisture it had already left on the table, and then rotated the glass with her fingers.

"What else would you like to know?" Henry prompted her.

"How did you wind up here?" Akira asked. She gestured around her, indicating the shabby kitchen. "Here, I mean. Rose once said that you'd never lived in the house, but it must have been important to you."

"This place?" Henry looked around the room, too. "I don't think so. Why I don't recall as I'd ever been inside the Harris place before I passed on."

Akira blinked. That made no sense at all. Ghosts who were tied to a place were always tied to a location that was important to them. Dillon was the only one she'd met who was linked to a car, but she'd encountered plenty of ghosts who were stuck in the place where they'd died. "But why are you here then?"

"I was looking for Rose," Henry answered. He picked up the newspaper from his lap, and unfolded it, opening it and flipping through the pages.

Akira waited, as Henry found what he was looking for. Smoothing down the paper, he folded it back up, this time with an article from a back page prominently exposed, and turned it, holding it out to her so that she could read it.

Akira glanced at the date at the top of the paper first. October 17, 1957. Her eyes skimmed down the page until she reached the tiny article that Henry's finger was pointing at. Rose Amelia Harris, in bold type, was followed by "age 19, died after a brief illness, on October 12. She is survived by . . ." but Akira stopped reading. She looked up at Henry.

"Your newspaper is about Rose?"

"From the day of her obituary, yes." Henry nodded, and took the newspaper back. He glanced down at the article, tracing over it with one finger. "I never knew what had happened to her. Her family didn't talk about it. Not to anyone. Her mama became almost a recluse after. And her little sister—well, Daisy left Tassamara just as soon as she could get away and she never came back. Not once."

"But Henry, that was decades ago," Akira protested.

"I never forgot her," Henry said. "Oh, I moved on. Got married. Had two fine boys. But Rose was my first love."

"And so when you died . . ." Akira prompted him.

"Right after is a bit fuzzy," Henry said reflectively. "There was this light."

Akira's eyes went wide. "A white light?"

"No, no. I'm not sure I'd call it white. No." Henry frowned, looking thoughtful. "Well, maybe. It was more like being in a cloud. But not a real cloud, not like fog, and not cold and wet. No, it was just . . . well, it's hard to describe. Can't say as I know the words to do it justice."

No ghost had ever told Akira anything like the story Henry was telling her. She was mystified. Was this what happened to people who didn't become ghosts?

"It was a pleasant enough place, but I was looking for Rose. I thought about her quite a bit at the end. I'd always wondered, always wanted to know. I'd been looking forward to seeing her. But I couldn't find her. And then, here I was. And here Rose was." Henry smiled. "It wasn't quite how I'd imagined meeting her again." He patted his belly ruefully. "If I'd known, I might have tried a little harder to lose a little weight before the end."

Akira smiled but she knew the expression didn't quite make it to her eyes. Henry must have recognized it, too, because he cocked his head to one side and asked, "Why did you want to know?"

Akira took a breath. "You're fading."

He shook his head, just slightly, as if to say he didn't understand.

"You're becoming like the boys." She gestured to the backyard. "Getting paler, more translucent. You're disappearing, Henry."

"Ah." He nodded, eyes turned to the window. "I see." He looked back at her. "There are worse fates, I suppose."

"Henry," Akira asked, a little desperately. "Is there a door? Or a passageway? A place where you should be going? A way back to that cloud? Because I think if you fade, it means . . . I think it means you're gone forever." Putting words to the fear for the first time was almost a relief.

Back before Daniel, she'd accepted the idea that ghosts were energy. Left-over energy. She thought of herself as a pragmatic scientist: she didn't believe in life after death, just that some people, perhaps with some kind of a unique quality to their body's electrical impulses, experienced a temporary transformation.

But Daniel and his father had gone somewhere, she was sure of it. And that meant that there was somewhere to go. Somewhere Henry ought to go, before he faded any further.

"Oh, yes," Henry said readily.

"Yes?" Although it was the response she hoped for, Akira was startled.

"It's not really a door," Henry said. "It's more like an opening. Like a hole almost."

"Like a tunnel?" Akira asked.

"Oh, could be." Henry appeared to be looking at something over her shoulder and Akira couldn't help turning to look. She saw nothing. She turned back to Henry as he shrugged. "I don't think I'd call it a tunnel, exactly. More just . . . a place. An entry."

"An air lock?" Akira asked, her curiosity getting the better of her.

Henry's eyebrows shot up. "I don't think it's an alien spaceship," he said. "It's not something from one of those movies Rose likes."

"Mystery Science Theater?"

"That's the show," Henry sighed. "I didn't think those movies were all that good the first time around. I don't really see why Rose needs to watch them again.

Akira had to smile, as Henry shook out his newspaper as if he was going to start reading again. "But Henry," she said hastily. "If there's a door, why don't you go through? It's got to be better than wasting away."

"Not without Rose." Henry turned a page of the paper.

"But Henry—" Akira began to protest. Didn't he understand?

"Not without Rose." Henry's answer was firm. "I'm not leaving her. Not again."

Akira frowned, then got up and went to the base of the stairs. "Rose!" she called up the stairs. Rose would be watching television, of course, but she never minded being interrupted. "Can you come down here, please?"

She returned to the table and took her seat again. Henry's newspaper was up, hiding his face, and Akira brushed her hand through it impatiently, shivering when the energy tingled her skin. She couldn't move the paper, the way she'd be able to if it was physical, but he'd be able to see her hand. "You can't hide," she said. "We're going to talk about this."

"Yes, Akira? What is it?" Rose popped into the room. "Are you going to say yes? Please? Pretty please?"

Akira sighed even as she smiled. "I've told you, Rose, I don't know enough people here to have a party."

"Just a little one," Rose suggested. "A little dinner party. You could make fried chicken. My mama's recipe is really good. I'll teach you."

Akira shook her head. "I'll think about it," she promised, as she did every time Rose brought up the subject. "But we have a bigger issue right now, and I need your help."

"Ooh, I get to help you?" Rose sounded surprised, but pleased. "What can I do?"

"You need to tell Henry that it's time to move on." Akira waved her hand through his newspaper again. "Put the paper down, Henry."

Rose's smile had faded. She stood in the center of the kitchen, looking uncertainly at the table where they were seated. "What do you mean?"

"Henry's fading," Akira told her, still looking at Henry. He was ignoring her. "But he says that he can see a way to go somewhere else. You need to tell him to go."

"But I don't want him to go!" Rose protested, planting her hands on her hips and glaring at Akira.

The room turned abruptly cooler, as if a breeze had just blown through. Oh, hell. Akira had been so focused on Henry that she hadn't thought about how Rose was going to react. She took a careful breath.

"Henry," she said cautiously. "Will you explain to Rose, please?"

Perhaps Henry could hear the note of fear in her voice, because he heaved a ghostly breath and put his paper down. Standing, he crossed to Rose and said mildly, "Now, Rose. Don't get all upset. I'm not going to leave you." He moved to put a comforting arm around her, but it passed right through her. She looked startled as he shook his head, and said, "Ah, right. Forgot."

"Henry?" Rose reached out to touch his face, but her hand just kept moving as if he wasn't there. She whirled to face Akira, snapping, "What have you done to him?"

Damn. Akira shivered. Rose was drawing in so much energy that the room was getting cold. The breeze had become a crisp winter wind. Akira measured the distance to the door with her eyes. She'd have to go straight through Rose to get there. Instead she pushed her chair back, a little closer to the wall.

"Hush, Rose," Henry interjected. "She hasn't done a thing. I've been like this for a while. You just haven't noticed."

"I—I didn't notice?" Rose's voice was tragic, her blue eyes wide. "Not notice you? Oh, Henry." Her lip wobbled, as if she was a child on the verge of tears.

"None of that, now." Henry waved a firm finger at her. "I don't mind so much. I'm sorry I can't touch you, but it's not so bad."

"He's fading," Akira said in a quiet voice. She didn't want to call Rose's attention to her, but Rose needed to know. "Like the boys in the backyard."

"The boys?" Rose looked to the door. "But they never come inside anymore. They used to be so much fun, but now—they never talk, they never even answer." She looked back to Henry. "Will you be like that?"

He shrugged. "Might could be. Can't say as I know, dear." Moving slowly, he returned to the table, his paper back in his hands.

Rose watched him, and then, subdued, said to Akira, "What can I do?"

"He has a way to go somewhere. A door. You need to convince him to take it."

"That thing?" Rose made a face.

"You see it, too?" Akira asked, surprised. "Why don't you use it?"

"Pfft." Rose waved off the suggestion. "It's been here ever since Henry got here, but I'm not going through that. I know what's over there. No, thank you." But then she paused and bit her lip. "But you should go, Henry," she said, sliding into a seat at the table, as Akira hastily shifted farther away. "It's different for you."

"Not without you, dear," he said, opening up his paper.

"That's just silly," Rose told him. "Why, Henry, on the other side of the door for you is heaven. St. Peter, pearly gates, streets of gold."

"Pearls," Henry said thoughtfully. He looked at Akira. "That's what that light was like. That color inside seashells, sort of white but real colorful at the same time."

Akira tried to imagine it, but picturing herself inside a seashell wasn't easy. She wanted to ask more questions—was it hard and shiny? He'd said it was like a cloud before. How could a seashell be misty? But it wasn't as important as what was happening to Henry.

"You're changing the subject, Henry. You need to move on. Otherwise, you're going to fade away. Either way, you'll be gone."

"I'm not leaving without Rose," he repeated stubbornly, not looking at either of them.

"Heaven, Henry," Rose told him again. "Eternal bliss. That's a lot better than fading away to nothing."

"We talked about this before, Rose. Back when I first passed. I'll go if you come with me. If not, I'm waiting right here until you're ready."

For the next few minutes, Rose and Henry argued. Or rather Rose tried to argue, and Henry repeated himself patiently. Finally, Rose seemed to give up. The pretty ghost was frowning, her face worried, but she didn't seem to have anything further to say. The three of them sat in silence.

Akira turned her glass a few times, studying it thoughtfully, before finally saying, in as gentle a voice as she could manage, "Rose? If you think it's heaven on the other side of the door, why don't you want to go there?"

"It won't be heaven for me," Rose said flatly. "Sinners burn in a pit of fire."

~CHAPTER FOURTEEN~

Akira didn't know what she believed anymore. Pits of fire sounded implausible to her, but then so did ghosts. Still, eternal damnation seemed awfully extreme for anything Rose could or would have done.

Henry must have felt the same way, because he didn't even pause before rejecting Rose's words. "God wouldn't damn you, Rose. Never. There's nothing you could do that his love isn't strong enough to forgive."

She looked at him, and her mouth twisted, and for a moment, it seemed as if she would stay silent. And then she said, "Pennyroyal tea."

The words meant nothing to Akira, but Henry looked taken aback. "Oh." He paused, then, with a reluctant curiosity, asked, "Who?"

"Tommy Shaw."

"Tommy!" Henry protested, almost recoiling. "He put a snake in your lunchbox!"

"I know that," Rose said, crossing her arms over her chest and looking defensive. "It wasn't even—I didn't—it wasn't—it had nothing to do with him, really."

"Well, why, then?" Henry sounded perplexed, his wrinkled face creasing into worried lines.

Rose sighed, giving a one-shouldered shrug. "I was just mad at my parents. They'd said such mean things to me about seeing you, I guess I figured I'd show them."

"Your pa would have made him marry you." Henry tilted his head, trying to understand.

"And then I would have been married to Tommy Shaw!" Rose's rejection of the suggestion brought her to her feet. "For the rest of my life? No, thank you!" She paced away, across the kitchen, skirt flaring around her from the strength of her movement.

Akira eyed her cautiously. There was no color change yet, just the chill in the air, and Rose still seemed in control. But emotional ghosts made her nervous. She looked at Henry. He was watching Rose, but he must have seen the movement of her head, for he looked back at her. Maybe he recognized her anxiety, because he changed the subject, saying to Rose, "I got him back for that snake."

Rose turned, and her smile lit up her face. "I knew that was you. How did you do it?"

"I got the janitor to let me in," Henry answered. "Old Mr. Jackson, he didn't mind. He thought it was funny."

"Mrs. Brown was so mad. She gave every boy in class detention. She knew it had to be one of them, but no one would own up to it."

Henry grinned back at her, and for a moment, Akira could see the boy he must have been. "I kept it real quiet after that. Didn't want to get beat up for getting them into hot water." And then seeing Akira's confused expression, he added. "Tommy Shaw put a garter snake in Rose's lunchbox one time. We must have been about thirteen, fourteen years old."

"Thirteen." Rose shuddered. "It was my brand-new Hopalong Cassidy lunchbox, and I was so proud of it. When I opened it up and that snake slithered out, I cried."

"I went down to the springs and caught some brown snakes. Nice big ones, a couple feet long. Harmless, but easy to mistake for cottonmouths. Stuck 'em in Tommy's desk. When he opened his desk, you could hear the screaming half a block away." Henry chuckled at the memory.

Rose smiled, too. "I wish I'd been remembering that snake when he asked me out. I might have thought twice."

A silence fell.

Akira gripped her glass tightly. She didn't want to ask but she had to. Henry's existence depended on it. "Pennyroyal tea?" she prompted cautiously.

"My parents would have sent me away. Everyone in town would have known. People always did." Rose's words were more sad than heated, and Akira took a deep breath, realizing for the first time that she'd been holding it. She understood now what the pennyroyal tea was for and what Rose had done, and she felt a pang of sympathy for the scared teenager Rose must have been.

"It doesn't matter," Henry said. "God can forgive anything."

"Well, I didn't ask to be forgiven," Rose responded with a toss of the head. "I died before I could have."

"First John 1:9 says 'If we confess our sins, he is faithful and just and will forgive us our sins and purify us from all unrighteousness.'" Henry answered. "It doesn't say anything about whether you have to be alive or dead when you confess."

"'The dead were judged according to what they had done,' Revelations," Rose snapped back. "I went to Sunday school every week, too, Henry Powell."

As the two ghosts argued about the Bible, Akira thought. She was convinced that fading away was bad. Maybe she was wrong: maybe slowly fading was just a gradual transformation. But if Henry became like the boys in the back, repeating the same actions as if on an endless loop, she felt some essential part of him would be lost forever. No, Rose needed to convince him to go through the hole or door or whatever it was.

But burning in a pit of everlasting fire? It didn't sound good. She could understand why Rose was reluctant to take the chance.

Still, if the Bible was literal truth, she'd be in that pit of fire, too, for the sin of communicating with ghosts. And yet what choice did she have? If there was a God and he didn't want her to see ghosts, he shouldn't have made so many of them. Asking her to stop meeting ghosts was like asking her to stop the tide: she just wasn't that powerful. But, wait—if there was a God, wasn't he all-powerful?

"No," she interrupted the ghosts, turning to Rose. "You can't be right, Rose. You won't go to hell. It doesn't make sense."

"The Bible doesn't have to make sense, it just is," Rose replied, as Henry frowned.

"Not the Bible." Akira waved that away. "Here's the thing: if God wanted you to burn in a pit of fire, you'd be there already. You've got a lot of energy, but you can't be more powerful than God, right?"

Rose looked doubtful, but Henry nodded eagerly. "That's right," he said. "There's no loophole that lets souls escape damnation. If you were damned, you'd be in hell already."

"Plus," Akira added, "If you take Henry through the door, you'll be saving his soul, and God would have to appreciate that. That has to outweigh anything bad you did while you were alive."

Rose frowned, and crossed back to the table. Standing next to them, she looked down on Henry. "Can't you go on your own, Henry?" she asked, her voice plaintive. "I like it here."

Henry stood, reaching for her hand, and then sighed as his hand went straight through her. "Rose, I had to leave you in life. Wasn't nothing I could do about it. But I loved you from the time I was a little boy, and I'm not leaving you behind now."

Akira bit her lip. Poor Henry. He was so sweet, so earnest, and the thought of him loving Rose his whole life made her eyes prickle as if she wanted to cry. Rose had to see that she couldn't just let him waste away.

"All right," Rose sighed. She looked over her shoulder and her chin lifted. "But if I wind up burning for eternity, I'm going to be very, very angry at you." She swallowed hard and Akira could see that she was mustering her courage. And then Rose turned, and with a sweep of her peach skirts, stepped away and was gone.

"Thank you, Akira." Henry's eyes sparkled and his shoulders straightened as if a huge weight had been lifted off his back. "Thank you so much. You take care now." He dusted himself off, tugging at his clothes as if to make himself look a little neater, and then he, too, stepped forward and was gone.

Wow. Akira sat, stunned. There was a door. And spirits could go through it. And she'd just helped ghosts move on to another place. It was amazing.

And then she realized what she'd done, and her mouth dropped open, and she jumped to her feet, saying, "Wait, wait. Henry, come back! Rose!!"

Oh, shit, she thought frantically. What about Dillon?

~CHAPTER FIFTEEN~

Dillon grieved.

Akira couldn't blame him.

The house was quieter, lonelier without Rose and Henry. Akira missed Henry's calm presence in the kitchen and Rose's lively charm, and it was worse for Dillon. The boys in the backyard were no company at all, so all he had was Akira.

He took to spending more and more time in his car.

"Grace bought you ten new Kindles, Dillon. Don't you want to come into the lab and try to fry them?" Akira asked in desperation one miserable day at the end of August. It was lunch time and she was sitting in the car, air conditioning at full blast.

Whoever had chosen this car had been an idiot, she thought wearily. A black car parked in the sun in Florida in August was an oven, and even with the air-conditioning, she felt as if she was baking. But it was even hotter outside the car, and she was worried about Dillon. She knew he could stretch to reach the lab if he wanted to, but he hadn't been willing to make the effort for days.

What she really needed, she thought, was a ghost psychologist.

"Maybe later," Dillon said from the backseat. "You should go in, though. It's hot out here for you."

"That's for damn sure," Akira muttered, checking the a/c settings for the third time. Maybe it was broken?

"Tell me again how it happened."

"Oh, Dillon." Akira partially turned to face him, leaning back and letting her head rest against the warm glass of the window. She felt sticky with sweat. "I've told you."

"When Henry died, he couldn't find Rose," he prompted her. "Start there."

Akira sighed. At least he didn't want to hear about the door again. She hadn't seen the door herself, so she couldn't really describe it, but she felt as if she'd spent hours trying to explain it to Dillon. And then he'd spent days trying to look over his shoulder, because of how she'd described Rose's way of looking at the door, as if it was somewhere behind her. It was almost as if he hoped he'd find it, just out of sight behind him.

"Henry was in a place that wasn't a cloud and wasn't foggy and wasn't a white light or a rainbow light," she started obediently, "but it looked something like mother-of-pearl, and he was trying to find Rose. He didn't tell me anything about how long he looked or what it was like to be looking for her, just that he couldn't find her. And then he was in the kitchen of the house."

Damn it, she thought, watching his face. Maybe she was the one who needed a shrink. Was she really making herself miserable worrying about a teenage ghost? But she couldn't help herself. She hated seeing him so unhappy. And even more, she hated not knowing how to help him.

"Do you think maybe my Gran is looking for me?" Dillon's words were almost casual, but his blue eyes were intent on Akira's. "Maybe that's why she's still here?"

What? Oh, hell. Oh, no. Is that what he was thinking? Over the course of the past few months, they'd almost stopped talking about the ghost in the Latimer house. Grace's researcher was still working, uncovering ever more obscure ghost stories, but Grace hadn't interviewed a new medium in weeks. Akira had been perfectly content to adopt an out of sight, out of mind philosophy when it came to that particular ghost.

"Even if she was," Akira said, trying to pick her words carefully. "There's nothing we could do about it." Dillon didn't look convinced and she sighed. "Dillon, there's no way to get close to a ghost like that. It'd be like walking into fire. The power will rip you apart."

"But maybe if she saw me, she'd calm down," Dillon said stubbornly.

"It doesn't work that way," Akira insisted. "Ghosts that have turned red, they're not thinking any more. They're just energy."

"You said it was like they were psychotic or hallucinating. You can talk to people who are hallucinating."

"Not if they're attacking you. The energy is destructive. You wouldn't be able to reach her."

"You said 'her.' You think it's my gran, too."

"What difference does it make?" Akira demanded.

"I've been thinking about it a lot," Dillon answered. "I want to go to see her."

"What? No!" Akira's response was immediate and instinctive. There was no way, absolutely no way, that she and Dillon were going anywhere near that house.

Five minutes later, she shivered in the cold. The only good thing about arguing with a ghost was that the more upset Dillon got, the cooler it got in the car.

"Well, there's nothing you can do about it," she finally said, feeling put-upon but triumphant as she pulled out her trump card. "You can't get there without the car, and I won't drive the car there."

"Fine, I'll walk," Dillon snapped at her. "I know the way." With an indignant push, he forced himself out of the car and started walking.

Akira watched him stomping across the parking lot, feeling self-righteously annoyed at him.

And then self-righteously annoyed and a little guilty.

And then a lot guilty and only a little annoyed.

It was his grandmother, after all. And he'd lost Rose and Henry. He was lonely. And being stuck in the car couldn't be fun. Maybe she should have found a nicer way to say no. But he was so stubborn!

With a quiet thunk, the passenger door opened, and Zane slid inside the car. "Hot day for this," he said. "Dillon, can't you make it into the lab? Make life a little easier on Akira?"

Akira shook her head. "He's not in the car."

"Oh?" Zane looked at her, the question clear.

"He's decided he has to go visit your mom," she said gloomily, watching Dillon's back as he crossed the parking lot. She wondered how far he'd get. She knew he'd managed to get several blocks away from the car: before she left, he and Rose had been having fun seeing how far up Millard Street they could get. There was a little park at the end of the street that they'd been trying to reach.

"Isn't that going to be tough?" Zane asked.

"Impossible, I think." Akira slumped a little in the seat, closing her eyes and leaning back against the headrest. Was Dillon suicidal? Could a ghost be suicidal? Maybe, if he was trying to destroy himself. If only she'd made Rose and Henry wait. If only she'd thought about Dillon, not just Henry. How could she have been so stupid? She berated herself silently, not for the first time.

A warm hand closed around hers and she opened her eyes,

startled.

"Talk to me," Zane said. "What's going on?"

Akira chewed her lower lip. How did she want to explain this?

"Stop that," Zane said. He leaned forward, dropping her hand, and sliding his hand up and around the back of her neck. He tugged her to him, gently, and she went with it, leaning into him as he took her mouth with his own, his lips and tongue caressing hers.

She felt the warmth rising in her veins, the rush of pleasure flowing through her. It had been months now, she thought fuzzily, and it was still the same—his touch, his taste, his smell, they hit all her triggers, more and more all the time.

He pulled away and she let him go reluctantly. "You're better than Xanax."

He chuckled. "Thanks. I think." He brushed his lips against hers again, and then prompted, "So, Dillon?"

"He has this idea that maybe your mom is like Henry, that she's trying to find him like Henry tried to find Rose."

Zane blinked. "Huh." He looked out into the parking lot thoughtfully. "That makes sense, actually. And it sounds like her."

"It sounds like her?" Akira repeated, not sure what he meant. They hadn't talked about his mom, not since that first night. She'd been so sure when he dropped her off at her house that it was over between them that steering clear of the subject had been almost instinctive. He'd been convinced that his mom would never hurt anyone; she'd been equally convinced that there was a dangerous ghost in his house. It seemed like a subject best avoided.

"Determined," he said. "She was Grace on steroids."

Akira couldn't help smiling at the image. Grace ran the company with a polite southern charm that did nothing to disguise the organized efficiency of her every movement. Grace on steroids?

"Scary?" she asked.

"Only if you were doing something she didn't like. But then, yeah. This one time—well, it's not important." Zane was smiling, as if it was a good memory, but he sobered as he went on. "I could definitely see her staying to try to find Dillon." He paused, opened his mouth as if he wanted to say something, then closed it again.

Akira bit her lip.

Damn it.

She knew what he wanted to say as surely as if she was the one who could read minds. Daniel and Rob and Henry and Rose had shown her that ghosts could or maybe should be going somewhere. She didn't know why Dillon couldn't find the way, but if Zane's mom was refusing to go without Dillon, then maybe . . .

"Ow. Hell." The voice from the backseat was disgruntled. Akira turned and Dillon glared at her. "I will get there," he said defiantly.

"Did it just get colder?" Zane asked, sounding startled as he reached to put his hand by the air-conditioner vent.

"Dillon's back and he's still mad at me," Akira reported matter-of-factly. Dillon crossed his arms over his chest and looked sulky as he leaned back in the seat and stared out the window.

Akira almost smiled. He would probably be annoyed if she told him he was cute when he was angry, but he was. His messy dark hair and pout made him look like a much younger child.

And then her smile faded as she realized that she wasn't scared of Dillon. Not in the least. He was angry at her, and she knew that made him dangerous, but she still wasn't scared.

Because she loved him. Somehow she had let a fifteen-year-old boy ghost who worried about everything slip under her defenses and enter her heart.

And then her eyes slid sideways to his uncle, who was watching her intently, eyes dark, slightly frowning, and she realized that she loved him, too.

He wasn't who she'd ever thought she'd want.

He barely cared about science. He wasn't serious. He wasn't intense. He didn't want to have deep, philosophical conversations about the meaning of life and how the universe might work. He'd rather watch baseball, one of the most boring sports ever invented.

But picnic tables and pool tables. Fire ants and Kindles. He might not make it obvious, but he paid more attention, noticed more, than anybody she'd ever met.

And this ghost—she was his mom. What would it be like, to know your mother was trapped in your house, lost in a ghostly vortex of despair?

Akira sighed. She thought she might be about to do one of the stupidest things she'd ever done.

If her father was still alive, he'd kill her for this.

❧

"Are you trying to kill me?" Zane's question was half rhetorical, half laughing. She always beat him at pool, but today she wasn't even pretending to give him a chance.

The crack of balls hitting one another, the soft whoosh of their slides along the green felt, the thumps as they dropped in the pockets had been the only sounds in Zane's office for at least twenty minutes. Akira's focus was complete. She was pointing out her shots with the cue, not bothering to call them, as she cleared the table, racked the balls, and cleared the table again.

It was as if he wasn't really there.

Or she wasn't.

"Hmm?" she answered, leaning over the table, eying the distances between the cue ball and the ten and the side pocket. And then she made another perfect shot.

Zane stuck his cue back in the rack. He didn't know what was going on in her head, but she wasn't playing. The casual game he'd started to finish out their lunch hour had turned into something else for her.

He returned to his desk. He'd get back to work and let her do her thing and eventually she'd break free from whatever thought had caught her and tell him what was happening. He'd seen this before. That time it had been right before she decided to give up on sonoluminescence and start researching spirit energy. It had been a tough decision for her since, despite her interest in the subject, it was essentially the death knell of any academic future.

This time, he thought it probably had something to do with Dillon and his mom. Akira had gone quiet in the car, right after they'd been talking about his two family ghosts. Her silence wasn't a surprise: they'd been avoiding talking about his mom for months now.

Accepting the existence of ghosts wasn't a stretch for Zane. Until that terrible week when he'd abruptly come face to face with the ugly reality of death, he hadn't put a lot of thought into what happened after, but his vague concepts of heaven or reincarnation or even an ending of everything were flexible enough to accommodate the idea of ghosts.

But his mom as a malevolent, murderous spirit? No way.

Just flat-out no.

It wasn't possible.

He hadn't wanted that difference of opinion to interfere with his interest in Akira, though. She fascinated him. He'd thought at first that it might be novelty. With her Japanese mother and Californian upbringing, she didn't look like the girls he'd grown up with.

And then he thought it was the surprise of the unexpected: she didn't act like the girls he'd grown up with either. When he was eighty years old, he'd still remember the pleasure found in friction turning kinetic energy into heat.

But it was more than either of those things now. She looked so fragile, but she'd stick her stubborn chin out and defend her point of view with vigor. She acted so serious and hard-working, but she was the best pool player he'd ever met, and he much preferred to have her on his team in Halo, rather than on the opposite side. And in bed . . .

Okay, he had to stop thinking about her while watching her play pool, or he'd never get any work done. But he was smiling as he checked his calendar. With any luck, he could clear out his email and they could cut out of here early. He could think of much better things to be doing with their time.

"All right," she said abruptly, an hour later, straightening, and lightly tapping the butt of her pool cue against the ground. "I'll do it."

"Do what?" he asked, looking over from his computer.

"Visit your mom," she responded, as if surprised by the question.

"Really?" Zane swiveled in his chair, turning to face her. "I thought you told Dillon no."

"He can't go see her on his own. It's too dangerous."

Zane leaned back. "Aneurysms? Murder by spirit energy? Remember that conversation?"

"Of course I do." Akira shrugged and looked away from him, as if something had suddenly become terribly interesting on the other side of the office.

"You said it was dangerous for you. What's changed?" Zane asked. She'd refused to go near the house for months. Why now?

"That medium probably had a weak spot in an artery already. The energy raised her blood pressure enough that it burst, but it wouldn't have killed her if the aneurysm wasn't already there," Akira answered.

Zane frowned. That didn't feel like an answer to the question.

"What if Dillon's right? What if she's looking for him?" Akira said.

Zane paused. This was his mom that they were talking about. He didn't like the idea that she was trapped in their house, unable to communicate with anyone, desperate and even violent. But he liked even less the idea of Akira risking her life.

"I'll have to go in first," Akira continued, looking thoughtful. "I'll calm her down before Dillon comes in."

"I'm not sure about this," Zane said. "Maybe we should talk to Nat first. See what she has to say."

"Dillon will have to wait in the car." Akira was planning now, strategizing as if she hadn't heard him.

"Yeah, I don't think I care about Dillon," Zane said.

"You should care," Akira protested. "Dillon's your nephew."

"And you're my lover," Zane answered her, exasperation in his voice. He wasn't going to let her distract him. "More dangerous doesn't mean not dangerous. Is this risky for you?"

Akira blinked at him. Once. Twice. Then she turned and busied herself putting away her pool cue.

"Besides, Dillon's dead already," Zane added. As soon as the words left his mouth, he wanted to kick himself. It was true, of course, but it wasn't what mattered. He'd been trying to work a conversation around to that "L" word—the one he'd never used with another woman—for weeks now and he'd never quite figured out how. He'd just had the perfect opportunity and he'd blown it.

"Which is why it's more dangerous for him." Akira turned back, her cheeks lightly pink, her eyes bright. "The energy would rip him apart."

"Uh, isn't an aneurysm like a blood vessel being ripped apart?"

Akira wobbled her hand in an equivocal gesture. "We can talk about it in the car."

☙CHAPTER SIXTEEN❧

She'd managed to sidestep the question.

"Is it risky for you?" Zane had asked.

Yes, it was risky for her.

And he really wasn't going to like what she had to tell him now. They were sitting in the car, this time in the driveway of the Latimer house. It was mid-afternoon, which in Florida, in August, meant that the sky was heavy with storm clouds. In the grey light, the house looked even more dangerous than it had before, a churning mass of energy.

She licked her lips. "All right, this is how it's going to work," she told Dillon. He was looking out the window at the house but at her words, he sat back.

"I don't see anything," he said, sounding disappointed.

Didn't see anything? Was he blind? For a moment, she wondered about the difference between her sight and what an actual ghost saw. That would be an interesting line of research if Dillon would cooperate. Maybe they could do some testing in her lab, try to set up some controlled energy experiments.

She was looking for something, anything, to focus on other than what she was about to do, she realized. It was a good plan—just the moment of scientific analysis had made her feel calmer—but getting distracted wasn't going to make this any easier.

"This is what we're going to do." She tried again. "You're going to wait in the car, Dillon, while Zane and I go in the house. You need to give us at least five minutes. I'm going to be trying to absorb some of the energy, enough of it to calm her down so that you can talk to her."

"Wait a minute, wait," Zane said. "Absorb the energy?"

Akira looked at him and forced a smile.

Oh, God, this was a really stupid idea, wasn't it? But she'd done things like this before. It wasn't so different, not really, from what she'd done with that angry religious ghost just a couple of years ago.

Almost subconsciously, she stretched out her hand, opening and closing the fingers.

It would be better to do it not quite the same way.

"It'll be okay," she told them both. "I won't be trying to take in all the energy, just enough that she calms down and you can talk to her, Dillon. So as you approach the house, go slowly and carefully. You need to think of it as like a whirlpool. If I haven't managed to break her out of the vortex, you're going to start feeling pulled. Don't give in to that pull—back off immediately!"

Dillon's blue eyes were wide. The intensity in her voice was getting to him, she saw. He wasn't scared, but he wasn't quite as eager as he had been just a few minutes ago.

"Just wait a couple of minutes and then give it another try." She looked from Dillon to Zane and back again, and swallowed. Zane wasn't going to like this, but she had to warn Dillon. "If you start feeling pulled from farther away—like if you're in the car, and it starts to feel like you're being tugged?—you need to get away. If that happens, go as far away from the house as you can."

"That would mean she's getting stronger?" Dillon asked. Akira let her gaze flicker to Zane. He was frowning.

"Yes, exactly."

"Why would she get stronger?" Dillon asked, sounding uneasy but fascinated.

She smiled tightly. "The obvious reason."

If the ghost managed to kill Akira, there'd be a lot more spirit energy in the vortex. Its reach would easily extend to the car, but if they parked too far away, Dillon would be stretching to get to the house.

Without waiting for him to figure it out, she hurried on. "Just remember what I said: wait and then approach slowly. If you feel pulled, run the other way. Okay?" As he nodded, she opened her car door and stepped out.

She took a deep breath as Zane joined her, then started walking, careful steps bringing her closer and closer to the house.

"What's the obvious reason?" he asked, voice grim.

Oh, dear. If he was bothered by that, he really wasn't going to like the rest of what she had to say.

"It's not important," she said. "There's something else you need to know. I didn't want to talk about it around Dillon." She glanced back at the car. Dillon's worried face was visible through the window.

Her mouth was dry and her legs had a quiver running down the back of them that meant her body was saying, run, run, run, but she'd made her decision.

And this was it, she realized. This was the conversation that always ended things.

She looked at Zane. His frown was almost a scowl, his eyes gone their grayest in the light. "Ghosts that have lost control pull in energy from the environment. Is there a room or a place in your house that's colder than it should be?"

Zane nodded. "Dillon's room. No one uses it, but it stays colder than the rest of the house."

"So we'll go there." Akira stepped up onto the porch. She was trying to think of some way to phrase this part of the story, some way to tell him the truth that would make it palatable for him. But there wasn't one, and she knew it, so before he could follow her up the porch, she turned. Their eyes were on the same level as she started talking.

"She'll try to take me over. Possess me," she said baldly. "That's what they do. I'll be trying to absorb her energy and fight her off at the same time. I'm pretty good at it, I've done it before." She glanced over her shoulder at the door. The energy almost made it look as if parts of the house were shifting and melting in her vision, but she knew that was just because of how she saw it. The house itself would be solid.

"Possess you?"

Was it disbelief in his voice? Akira wasn't sure but she pressed her lips together for a moment and then continued steadily, trying not to remember the sympathy in the voice of the boyfriend in college who had told her she needed psychiatric help.

"The thing is, she's really strong. It's going to feel to me like I'm being electrocuted. I can take it for a few minutes, but unless I can bleed off a lot of her power, enough to bring her back to rationality, it probably won't be in time."

"In time for what?" His voice held a snap.

"In time for—" Akira paused. "Look, spirit power is like electricity. It'll cause random electrical activity in my brain. That's going to cause seizures. I can't tell you what they'll look like. If they're mild, you might not even notice, but they might be more serious."

"Meaning what?"

"Ah, well, um, convulsions, basically. You know, the full-bore, falling down, jerking and twitching, unconsciousness thing." She tried to smile again but he didn't smile back.

"Here's what matters," she continued quickly. "Ghosts get stronger from blood, so it's really important that I don't bleed. If I start losing blood for any reason, I'll get weaker, and she'll get stronger. That would be bad." Zane was starting to shake his head no, even as she kept going, "But ghosts hate pain. Once they're dead, they don't have any physical sensation and they forget what it's like. If you—if I get hurt, she's likely to let go of me, at least for a bit."

Zane's head motion stilled, and he reached for her, putting a hand on either shoulder. Akira could feel the warmth through the light cotton of her shirt and she tried to let it soothe her, but the tension in her muscles didn't ease.

"I don't know what you're saying, but I don't like it," he said.

"Since my dad died, I've only done this once. That time, I—" She was opening and closing her hand, she realized, almost convulsively, and with a deliberate effort, she stilled herself. "I took a hammer and I broke my hand."

His fingers closed around her shoulders, squeezing hard. It wasn't painful, just tight. "It's tough to judge how hard to hit," she said. "My dad . . . my dad. . ." How could she explain this? But she didn't have to.

"You had convulsions, and your father, instead of taking you to a hospital, beat you until he broke your bones?" Zane interrupted, and this time the emotions in his voice were unmistakable. Shock. Horror. Revulsion.

"I've been possessed by ghosts and my father saved my life by hurting me, yes." Akira wanted to cry, but she tried to keep her voice even. "And broke a few bones along the way, that too," she added, the admission almost reluctant.

"Akira, that's insane!"

"I know what it sounds like." Akira almost laughed, although not with humor. "If I'm not schizophrenic, I've got post-traumatic stress. Abused child hallucinates as a defense mechanism, rationalizes the abuse to avoid perceiving herself as a victim, her father as a villain. There's no such thing as ghosts and I ought to be locked up for my own safety."

Zane let his hands fall off her shoulders. "Let's not do this," he suggested.

Her chin went up. "Look, if you think I'm crazy, no big deal. We walk through your house, nothing bad happens, we walk back out." She shrugged.

"I don't think you're crazy." His defense sounded automatic, not quite sure. He touched her cheek. "But I don't—look, have you ever seen a shrink?"

Her smile didn't reach her eyes.

"Just to be sure?" he continued. "Just to . . . your father beat you. He broke your arms, your ribs, your jaw. Because you had seizures! Anyone would be traumatized by that. There's nothing wrong with getting help."

"Any decent psychiatrist would lock me up." She said the words softly, gently. Her tears were very close to the surface but she held them back by force of will. She would not cry, not now.

"Let's go back to the office. Let's talk to Nat. She's a doctor. Maybe she can help."

Akira shook her head. She glanced back at the car, at Dillon, who had gotten out and was sitting on the roof, watching them, frowning. "I want to help Dillon," she said. "He needs this. And I—I love him." She paused. Then she shook her head and turned toward the door. "Let's just do it. We'll walk through the house, you'll show me Dillon's room. End of story."

Zane unlocked the door, torn between insisting that they go see Nat and letting Akira have her way.

Could she have fooled him? Could she be delusional? Could the ghosts she saw simply be hallucinations, products of a traumatized mind?

She wouldn't have deceived him maliciously. There was no way he would believe that. But part of his job as head of GD's special affairs division was to hire people with psychic abilities, the ones who worked on GD's special projects. He knew many people with gifts, but he'd also met some incredibly skilled fakes.

Could Akira have an innate, even subconscious, ability to do a cold read that had been good enough to trick him? And the rest of his family?

He led her through the foyer and straight up the stairs to the second floor, his brain churning. He was trying, for the moment, to set aside his horror at the idea that her father, the man who should have been protecting her, had been beating her instead. Beating her because she had seizures!

Back when he'd first learned about the broken bones, he'd sort of assumed that her father had abused her. Natalya had said most of the breaks happened long ago, and even he realized that most abused children are abused by their parents. But every time she'd mentioned her father, it was with such obvious affection and love that he'd stopped thinking about it. Maybe he should have tried harder to learn about her past, but he hated it when she stiffened up. It had been easy, too easy, to let it slide, to not ask painful questions.

Zane was fiercely glad that the man was dead. He wanted more than anything right now to find him and hurt him like he'd hurt Akira. But he needed to let that go, he knew. He wouldn't know how to help Akira in the here-and-now until he understood what was going on. Did she really have a gift that let her see ghosts or was she insane? In the back of his mind, a thought was pushing at him, fighting to rise to the surface, but he ignored it, trying to focus.

She'd known Dillon's name. But it wouldn't have been hard to find that out. Anyone in town might have shared information about the Latimer family on her first visit without thinking anything of it. Rose's name, though, that would have been harder to learn. Zane had looked it up soon after Akira had moved in, and a teenage girl named Rose Harris had died at that address back in the 1950's.

But even though the name was right, how could Akira have learned it casually? Or by accident? It seemed almost impossible.

When he'd been reading about ghosts, there'd been an article about people who believed they were possessed. The symptoms fit into the same diagnostic group as people with multiple personalities. "Dissociative identity disorder," he said aloud.

"What about it?" Akira asked, as she caught up with him at the top of the stairs.

He looked down at her pale face and tried not to frown. Could she have multiple personalities? Really? She'd never behaved erratically, never acted like a different person. But to know Rose's name, she would almost have to have researched it. "You could have that," he offered. "Multiple personalities. It was in an article I found about ghosts."

She raised her eyebrows. "Great," she said. "Good to know."

He sighed and gestured toward the door of Dillon's bedroom.

But say she had multiple personalities, his thoughts continued. She would still have to be an incredibly gifted cold reader. She'd known such subtleties. How could she have found out Dillon's musical taste? She couldn't have, which meant that it had to be a guess, but a perfect guess. What could have clued her in?

Akira stepped forward. He was watching her intently, still trying to think through the implications of what she'd told him, still trying to analyze every experience of ghosts that they'd had together over the past several trusting months, so he saw the movement of her throat as she swallowed, and the seemingly involuntary shudder of her shoulders as she placed her hand on the door.

"Seizures, by the way?" she said, not looking at him. "Five continuous minutes will damage neurons. Thirty minutes has a decent chance of killing me." She turned the knob, and pushed the door open, and stepped into the room, just as his thoughts crystallized around an idea: door, ghosts, North Carolina, bodies.

Hell.

Sure, some skillful guessing might have gotten her a lot of information about Dillon and some research might have provided her with Rose's name. But she'd found two bodies in North Carolina that the local police and the FBI had spent days searching for. That wasn't just a lucky guess.

"Let's not do this," he started, following her into Dillon's bedroom. "At least let's talk about it a little more."

But it was too late.

Akira's head arched back as if she'd just been hit in the face, and her whole body went stiff, then she crumbled forward, falling against the floorboard of the bed and then to the ground as if she was a marionette whose strings had just been cut.

"Akira!" He jumped to her side, just as the thought that had been pushing at the back of his mind jumped full-blown to the forefront: if she wasn't insane, she wanted him to rescue her from ghostly possession by hurting her.

Hurting her badly enough to break her bones.

That's what he should have been paying attention to. That's what he should have been worrying about. Wondering whether she was crazy was just a way of avoiding thinking about what she wanted him to do.

He turned her over gently. She'd hit the bed exactly wrong. Blood was running from her nose, he realized, just as her muscles started to spasm.

Fuck.

The ghost would get stronger.

She wanted him to hurt her.

She needed him to hurt her.

And he didn't think he could do it.

ര്യ

Every step up the stairs took an effort. It was like walking through a red-tinged blizzard only instead of heavy snowflakes pelting across her skin, tiny shocks of static were penetrating deeper and deeper as she got closer to the door. She felt as if she were being flayed, but knew no sign of it would show.

This was such a bad idea. What was she doing, braving a malevolent ghost? This wasn't her—she was a coward! She couldn't even tell Zane she loved him, but she thought she could face this?

Walking through the doorway and into Dillon's room felt like moving from a snowstorm to an ice storm. She had time for a quick glimpse at a pleasant boy's room: wide windows, blue walls, overstuffed bookshelves, a world map with pins in it above a neat desk. And a woman standing at the end of the bed, streaked blonde hair in a perfect chin-length bob, fair skin, laugh lines, a trim figure—she looked enough like Grace that Akira would have known her instantly anywhere—but her face was bereft with grief and the red energy surging around her lashed out at Akira like lightning striking.

Akira's scream strangled in her throat. She felt herself falling, crashing, burning. The sharp physical pain of hitting her face almost broke through the agony of passing through the woman's ghostly energy.

For a moment, the shock was almost relaxing. The stunning pain left her brain fuzzy. But then as Zane turned her over, she began resisting the energy, trying to absorb some of it while holding the rest at bay.

The convulsions started immediately.

Her back arched, her jaw clenched, her muscles spasmed.

She was drowning in spirit energy. It was pouring in on her, drenching her in power.

Akira was fighting for control of her body, but so was the ghost.

The pain was intense. But she could also feel Zane's strong arms holding her, and a dull throbbing from her face and a warmth trickling down her chin. What was that?

She could hear Zane's voice. He was swearing steadily as he shifted her. What was he doing?

But she could also hear the ghost. She was screaming in pain, despair, an agony of her own. "I can't find you! Max? Dillon? Help me, help me!"

Akira tried to answer her, tried to open her mouth and form words, but a taste, a warm metallic flavor, distracted her. Shit. That was blood.

She opened her eyes, trying desperately to see even as Zane put something up to her face and her contracting muscles tried to pull her in three directions at once.

He was trying to stop the bleeding, she realized dimly. With something cotton. It smelled of him.

She could see his frantic face, hear the worry as he cursed, but most of her sight was taken up with the tornado of red energy surrounding his mother's ghost. She was getting stronger, Akira realized. Oh, that was bad.

And now she could hear another voice, too.

Dillon.

Screaming her name.

And then he popped through the bedroom wall next to the window and Akira, desperately struggling to take in only the energy she could handle, realized he was caught in the vortex.

Oh, hell.

Akira stopped fighting. She let the energy pour through her, filling her body, enveloping her in spirit power.

But it still wasn't enough.

So she let go.

❧

Five minutes? That was what she'd said, five minutes until neurons died.

Zane had ripped off his t-shirt and was holding it to Akira's face, trying desperately to stop the bleeding.

Fuck, fuck, fuck.

She'd taken a hammer and broken her hand.

She wanted him to do the same. Maybe not the hammer part, but the breaking part.

Could he do it?

But even as he thought the question, her body relaxed, her muscles loosened, and the seizure ended.

Thank God, he thought fervently, looking down at her as she blinked a few times and shook her head. That must not have been as bad as she expected.

"Zane? Honey?" she said, looking confused, and putting a hand up to her face to push his t-shirt away. "I just had the worst dream."

Zane froze. The words were wrong. But so was the voice.

She was already pushing herself to a sitting position when he asked, "Mom?"

"Oh, honey." Akira put her hand to her temple, squeezing her eyes closed, as if she had a pounding headache. "What are you doing here?"

"Mom?" Zane repeated himself, as he crouched next to her in the dim light of the bedroom. "Tell me something that only you would know." He didn't want to believe this. This couldn't be his mom. It wasn't possible. And it was more than impossible, it was flat-out creepy. Could his mom's ghost really have just taken over his girlfriend's body?

She shook her head and laughed faintly. "What?"

"Please, just tell me something that only you would know."

She looked at him and they were Akira's eyes, the brown so dark it was almost black, nothing like his mother's eyes. But the expression was wrong.

Just wrong.

"You've always been my favorite?" she offered.

His answer was a choked laugh. Now that was right. Not that he was his mom's favorite, but that she'd say so, in just that way.

"You say that to all your kids," he answered automatically. She did. Routinely. Sometimes even in front of one another.

But it wasn't good enough. A good fake, a good cold reader, could have gone for just that soft spot. Every kid wanted to believe that he was his mother's favorite. And if it was wrong, it would still make the mark happy.

"Try again. Something only you would know."

She shook her head, and then brought up her other hand, so that she was pressing both temples, expression pained. "I don't know, honey. I can't . . . Shouldn't you be off with Lucas? I thought you had that job in Paris this week."

He stilled. His mother had been a sensitive subject between him and Akira. He'd never talked to Akira about his mom's death after those first conversations. And who else would have? How would Akira have known that he and Lucas were in France when Dillon died?

Now that he had the truth, he didn't want it.

"Oh, but . . ." she started and then she stopped. She looked at him for a second, face still, and then she curled in around herself, hands covering her face, shoulders hunching down, legs drawing up, as if she was trying to make herself as small as possible.

She hadn't done that in life. He'd seen her two days after Dillon died and she'd been stoic. Upright, perfect posture, face composed, taking care of business. And death had a lot of business attached to it: funeral homes, newspapers, plans for a service, communications with friends and neighbors.

He touched her shoulder, feeling helpless. It was old pain to him. But her grief was throwing him back into that moment. Zane had missed the police investigation and the expedited autopsy, but he and Lucas had arrived in the middle of the planning stages, just barely in time to see their mother before the stroke that killed her, and then take over the planning for a joint memorial service.

Well, Lucas and Grace had taken over the planning, anyway. Zane had spent a lot of time playing foosball with his dad.

"What?" Her head shot up. "Dillon?"

Scrambling to her feet, she hurried over to the window, reaching out as if to embrace an invisible figure. And then she recoiled. "What the hell?"

She looked back at Zane, and then back and forth between the window and him as he stood, stuffing his hands in his pockets.

"Dillon's dead," she said. It wasn't quite a question.

"Yeah." He answered her. Dillon wasn't the only one who was dead, though. Should he tell her?

"What?" she said again, looking down at herself in shock.

Hmm. It looked as if Dillon was telling her for him.

"Oh, my God." The horror in her voice was so like his mother's tone when she got offended over something in the newspaper that Zane almost wanted to laugh. He could practically see her throwing the paper down by her bowl of breakfast cereal and swearing she'd never again vote for whatever local politician had annoyed her.

"This is not okay," she snapped. "What were you thinking?"

"Me?" she continued, and then she looked puzzled. "Really? I suppose. Oh!" And then her eyes grew wide and her hand flew up to cover her mouth. "I thought that was a dream."

Zane glanced at the clock on Dillon's bedside table. It was blinking. No one had bothered to reset the time after the last power outage. How long had it been already? And did this count as a seizure? Were Akira's five minutes still ticking down?

"Mom," he said. "You really need to go."

But then he stopped.

This was his mom. He'd missed her so much. The whole family had grieved for her and still grieved. Every anniversary, every birthday, every holiday was as colored by her absence as it had been shaped by her presence in life.

But still, every minute might be putting Akira in more danger.

She looked confused. "I should talk to your father."

"No." Zane's reaction was immediate and strong, but instinctive. He didn't know where it came from, but he repeated himself. "Mom, no."

"Why?" She touched her forehead again, pressing her fingertips against it.

Zane took a step closer to her, feeling helpless, unsure, but trying to find the words to say what he felt sure was true. A rumble of thunder sounded from outside.

"He misses you every day," he finally said. "Every day. If you talk to him now, today, it'll be the best day of his life. But then tomorrow, it'll be the worst day of his life all over again. And you could be hurting Akira by being in her body like that. You can't stay long enough to talk to him. You have to go. And really go this time. Look for a door or a passageway or something and go through it. And take Dillon with you."

Her lips firmed and she frowned.

"Mom," Zane said, feeling desperate. "Akira told me how to get you out. Ghosts don't like pain, she said. If I hurt her badly enough, if I beat her, you'll let go of her body. Don't make me do that." He didn't even try to disguise his horror at the idea.

"Huh," his mom said. "I gave birth to four children without painkillers. Nothing you could do is going to hurt more than that." But then her gaze softened as she saw his expression. "And you couldn't do it anyway, honey."

"Probably not," he admitted. If he closed his eyes and tried to pretend he was playing baseball, swinging a bat? But no. No amount of pretense would make a difference. "I can't. So please don't make me try, Mom. Please just let go of her."

She sighed. She looked around the room, and then at the doorway, and she seemed to be listening. "I'm really very angry," she said, but she didn't sound angry, she sounded sad.

Zane glanced at the clock again. Two more minutes had passed.

"How could you?" His mom said, but it was clear that she wasn't talking to him. Come on, Dillon, Zane thought fervently. Convince her to let go.

"All right." She turned back to Zane and her smile—it was his mother's smile, the wry half-amused, half-annoyed smile she showed when she signed his report cards, littered as they were with comments like, 'Could be an A student if he ever turned in his homework' and 'A pleasure to have in class, but needs to apply himself.'

"Tell your father that if I'm moving on, he should, too," she said briskly. "And tell your sisters that I still want more grandchildren, even though I'm not here to nag them about it. Tell Lucas . . ." She paused and Akira's eyes filled with tears, but then she continued. "Tell Lucas I'm sorry I failed him."

"Oh, Mom," Zane's words were a murmur. She probably didn't hear them over whatever Dillon said, though, because her impatient wave didn't look directed at him, as she added, "He trusted me to take care of you."

A flash of lightning was followed by a quick crash of thunder, and the soft drumbeat of the skies opening.

"All right, already," she said, sounding exasperated. "Moving on."

She looked at Zane and her smile warmed. "I love you, baby. Be happy."

"Love you, too, Mom," he answered, the choke in his voice not enough to block the clear, strong words.

And then Akira's face went blank, and her body swayed. Zane jumped forward, catching her before she fell again.

Thank God, he thought again. Thank God. His sisters and brother, his dad, they might be furious with him for not letting them have a chance to say good-bye, but he had to talk to Akira. He had to tell her he was sorry for doubting her, sorry for questioning.

Although he still wasn't convinced about that pain thing. It wouldn't have worked on his mom, he was sure of it.

But Akira didn't push herself up and away from him. She didn't speak up in the cranky, annoyed tone that she used when she showed weakness. She didn't do anything.

"Akira?"

Was she breathing?

Her body was a dead weight in his arms, her soft hair brushing his chin. "Akira?" he repeated, sharper this time. He tried to turn her, but she was sliding, her legs not holding her, her body limp and heavy. He side-stepped two steps trying to keep her upright, but her feet were slipping so he bent his knees, bringing her gently to the ground, supporting her head as she dropped to the carpet.

"Akira?" He tried for a third time, but there was no response, not even a flutter in her eyelids. He glanced at the clock again. How long had it been? But the light of the clock was gone. Damn. The power was out.

"Akira!" he snapped. And then he reached for her neck, for the soft crevices next to the strong tendons, feeling for the beat, for the steady thud of her working heart.

Nothing.

He took a deep breath and tried to still his own panic. Maybe he was touching the wrong spot. He shifted his fingers, and tried to calm himself, and tried to listen, and tried not to let his unruly thoughts take control. But . . .

Still nothing.

Her heart wasn't beating.

She was dead.

CHAPTER SEVENTEEN

Whoa.

That ghost had been strong.

Akira found herself pulled out of her body and thrown into nothingness without a pause.

She looked around and knew, with a touch of wry humor to the thought, that she'd just screwed up big-time.

She understood why Henry had had a tough time describing this place.

It wasn't really a place. It didn't feel solid, not like she was used to solid. Not so much that she thought she'd fall, but more that if she tried, she thought she could move in any direction, down or up or sideways. And not that she was floating, at least not floating like a balloon, but maybe as if she was floating in something like water, safe and supported but not constrained. Enclosed but not limited.

And the white? It wasn't really white. But maybe it was a very colorful white? Like white with glints of vibrancy that showed up at the corners of her vision so that it almost seemed that if she could turn in just the right way, she'd be inside a rainbow of color?

And the cloudiness? It was sort of more like cloudy vision than actually being in a cloud, as if everything—which was nothing—was out of focus.

It felt like a dream. Only not a dream.

And then a firm hand grabbed her wrist from behind, and Akira stumbled as she was pulled, away and down and backwards.

"We are not staying," Rose said, voice as firm as her grip.

"Wait!" Akira protested. "What about my parents? Shouldn't I see them?"

Rose waved a hand in the cloud as if to brush away the idea of meeting Akira's parents and kept moving. "They'll be there when you go back. There's no rush, you know."

And then it was too late. They were back in the room she'd just left.

"What the hell?" Akira demanded. She'd wanted to meet her mom. Her only memories were so fuzzy and indistinct. And she'd wanted to see her dad, too. Their relationship hadn't always been easy, but he'd loved her. She wanted him to know that she was doing okay without him.

Although dying probably wasn't the best way to show him that.

"Not hell," Rose replied, shaking out her skirt, and then patting her hair into place. "But we don't want to be there."

"Rose!" Dillon exclaimed from the doorway. "And Akira?" He sounded doubtful as he said her name, Akira noticed, so she looked down at herself. Had she changed? Nope, same old self.

"That doesn't seem good," said Zane's mom.

"No," Dillon agreed. Both of them were looking from her to Zane and back again. His back was to her, and he was kneeling on the other side of the bed, closer to the window so Akira crossed to his side and looked down.

She looked pale, she noticed dispassionately. And not terribly healthy. Maybe Rose was right and she needed a new shade of lipstick.

"Breathe, Akira, breathe," Zane was saying.

Oh, dear.

Akira tried to breathe experimentally.

It felt like she was breathing. Her chest moved as if her lungs were absorbing and releasing oxygen. But she couldn't feel any air shifting through her mouth or nose. She held her hand up to her face and tried to blow. Nothing.

"But, Rose, what about Henry?" Dillon was saying behind her.

"Henry's fine," Rose answered. "His wife was a touch unhappy that he'd waited for me, but she's getting over it. Quick, Akira, go get back in your body."

"How?" Akira asked. She didn't seem to feel any kind of a pull toward her body. It was strange watching it, but it didn't really feel as if it belonged to her anymore. It was just there.

"Maybe if you lie on top of it?" Dillon suggested.

"Just put it on like clothes, you think?" Akira asked. It didn't sound appealing, but she was willing to give it a try. She stepped over her body, then, feeling silly, lay down on top of it, moving through Zane's hands and arms as if they weren't there.

Moving through a human was strange. She'd always felt it when ghosts moved through her: that tingle of spirit power, the sizzle of feeling. But she felt nothing moving through Zane.

And nothing moving through her own body, either. She wiggled experimentally and waited.

Still nothing.

"Not working," she reported from her position on the ground. She could see the ghosts, standing behind Zane, but most of her attention was focused on his face.

"I'm so very sorry about this," Zane's mom said to Akira. "I had no idea."

Akira nodded, still watching Zane. He was giving her CPR now, rhythmically pushing on her chest, as he chanted under his breath, "Come on, come on, come on."

"I knew it was dangerous," Akira said. "I thought I'd be able to absorb enough of the energy to bring you back to consciousness. Sort of like ghostly detox. Then Dillon could have talked to you and you both could have moved on together."

"Moved on?"

"Through the passage," Rose interjected. "Can you see it?"

As the ghosts fell into conversation behind Zane, Akira watched his face. In the dim light, she could see beads of sweat forming at his temples. With the power out, the room must already be heating up.

Some part of her had been waiting for the end, but this wasn't how she'd thought it would come.

She'd imagined he'd get tired of her, find her too crazy, move on the way guys always did. Oh, maybe in the beginning it had been just as likely that she might find his irreverent attitude annoying and become so prickly that he'd retreat in self-defense, but she'd known for weeks now that that wasn't going to happen.

She liked him too much. When she got prickly, he knew just how to make her laugh. When she was anxious and fretful, he knew just how to soothe her. When she was with him, she forgot to be scared.

Of course, that wasn't necessarily a good thing, she realized.

"Did he hit me?" she asked abruptly, interrupting the ghostly conversation about passageways.

"What?" "No." "Of course not!" The answers came all at once, Rose surprised by the question, Dillon matter-of-fact, Zane's mom shocked and maybe even a little offended.

She hadn't thought so.

She rolled out of her body, sitting up, but staying where she could see his face. He looked both desperate and determined, his attention focused on his hands, one over the other, forcing her heart to pump, her blood to circulate.

She felt safer with him than she'd ever felt in her entire life, she realized.

It was an odd realization to come to while crouched over her dead body.

But he would never hurt her. Never crack her ribs, never twist her arm until the bone fractured. Never smack her to make her see things his way.

"Start breathing, babe," Zane ordered her, without pausing his movements. Akira trailed her ghostly hand over his lower arm, stroking the taut muscles. She couldn't feel him, and she knew he couldn't feel her. And if she pushed just a little harder, her hand would pass right through his arm. But touching him was still comforting.

One hundred compressions a minute was the current standard for CPR, and it looked as if he was aiming for that. But how long could he keep up the pace? It was physically demanding work.

"I'm calling 911. I know you hate hospitals," he threatened her.

Uh-oh. She'd died here. If an ambulance took her body away and she was trapped in the house, then it was game over. She'd never get back.

"Um, guys? A little help here?" Akira interrupted the ghosts again. Zane was pulling his phone out of his pocket, and if she didn't figure out how to stop him from calling 911, she might be in big trouble. "We've got to stop Zane from calling an ambulance."

Well, she was in big trouble no matter what. But worse trouble if her body headed off to a hospital without her.

Damn it, damn it, he was already pressing buttons. No, no, no, she thought furiously. Zane gave a convulsive shudder and his fingers paused.

"Akira?" he asked. "It just got colder. Bad idea?"

Oh, great. Communication via temperature change. For just a second, Akira tried to envision how she could use that ghostly ability to talk to Zane. Then she realized that another ghostly ability might be more useful.

"Can you fry the phone, Dillon? Like the Kindles?" Akira asked.

She might not be able to talk to Zane but she could stop him from calling out.

"Yeah, probably," Dillon answered her. "But how does that help you get back in your body? He should call an ambulance. You need medical help. You need to get to the hospital."

"What if I'm tied to the house?"

All the ghosts started speaking at once.

"But if you're not—" Dillon began.

"Should I try to take over your body again?" Zane's mom asked. "Just to get your heart beating?"

"If your body starts up, maybe your spirit will get pulled into it," Rose suggested. "No matter where you are, I mean. Or the parts of you."

Akira pressed her hands to her head, trying to think. She felt almost panicky. Every option seemed dangerous. But what could she do? How could she get back in her body? If other ghosts could possess her, how could she possess herself?

Zane had set the phone down next to him, and was back to giving her chest compressions. He was concentrating, focused, staring at her still face for any hint of motion. The cold from Akira's moment of panic must have faded, because he was dripping with sweat now, rivulets running down his bare chest.

Akira took a deep breath. She couldn't feel it, but just as it had been for Rob, it was calming anyway.

"Dillon and Rose," Akira said, steady now. "Work on the phone. Try to send him a text message."

"But how?" Dillon protested. "I can't control the power. I just zap things."

"The same way Rose picks numbers on the remote control," Akira answered. "If you can choose a number for a television station, you ought to be able to choose a letter on a cell phone."

"But I'm not strong enough," Rose said. "I can only make it change a couple of numbers at a time."

"Work together. Dillon, instead of trying to control the phone, just try to push energy through Rose. Let her control it."

The two ghostly teenagers looked at each other and shrugged, then crowded a little closer to Zane and his phone and started talking to one another.

Akira pushed herself to her feet and pulled Zane's mom to the side. She'd been watching Zane, too, looking almost as worried as Akira felt. "Tell me how you took over my body."

"I really am very sorry about that," the older ghost started.

Akira shook her head, dismissing it. "It's not important. How did you do it? If you did it, I ought to be able to do it, too. I just need to learn how."

Zane's mom bit her lip. "It's like trying to remember a dream. A very bad dream."

"Anything could help." Akira could hear the edge of desperation in her voice.

"It was almost like I was caught in a storm on the ocean. Not rain so much, but wind tossing me around and darkness. I was calling for help, looking for something, anything, to hold onto when suddenly there were lights. Two of them, one bright blue, the other yellow."

She frowned, and shook her head, her blue eyes far away. "I knew the yellow one was Zane, even though it was just a light. I tried to catch him, but it was impossible, like holding light would be. I couldn't do it. But then I grabbed for the blue light, and it was solid. Soft, though."

Zane's mom was gesturing with her hands, as if she was trying to demonstrate how she had tugged on the light. "I could hold it, almost as if it was a pillow or a blanket. I dug my fingers in, and hung on, and tried to wrap it around me, and then . . ." Her eyes returned to Akira, and a wry smile pulled up one corner of her mouth, as she added, a hint of apology in her voice. "I woke up in your body."

"A blue light?" Akira looked back at her body. Zane hadn't given up, she saw gratefully, and neither had Dillon and Rose. They were hovering over his shoulder, holding hands, with Rose touching the phone.

"I've never used one of these," Rose was saying. "There aren't any buttons. How do I—oh, I see."

But there was no blue light, nothing for Akira to grab onto. How much time had already passed? How much longer did she have left before the lack of oxygen to her brain made it impossible for her to return to her body?

"But I—I mean, my body—it was fine when you were in it, right? No pain?"

"Oh, I had a terrible headache," Zane's mom responded promptly.

Shit. A ruptured cerebral aneurysm could cause a headache. Blood would be seeping into her body from the burst blood vessel, hemorrhaging steadily.

No blue light.

A terrible headache.

There was only one possible conclusion: she was dead.

She felt suddenly numb, almost cold. Moving slowly, she sat down on the bed. "You can stop now, guys," she said to Dillon and Rose.

"No, no, we've almost got it," Dillon said, eyes bright with excitement as he glanced at her. "We've figured out how to get the letters working."

"It doesn't matter." It was hard to get the words out. Akira thought she ought to be shouting, screaming, raging, but she didn't feel it. It wasn't anyone's fault, not really.

Zane's mom hadn't meant to kill her.

Dillon hadn't understood the danger.

Zane hadn't even had a chance to save her—except for the endless moments of cardiopulmonary resuscitation.

She'd taken a risk and it hadn't paid off.

But oh, she wished she'd told Zane she loved him.

She still could, she supposed. If Dillon and Rose could use the phone, she could have them text her message to Zane. What would she say? Apologize? Tell him he was the best thing that ever happened to her? Or just a simple, "I love you. Good-bye."

Her eyes closed. She wasn't ready. She didn't want this. Somewhere, behind the numbness, a huge reservoir of pain was about to open up and flood her, Akira knew.

"Don't give up!" Zane's mom had been watching her and stepped forward. "Whatever you're thinking, you could be wrong."

If she let go, if she let the despair sweep through her, what would happen? Would she become the next red vortex ghost in this house, destroying the others in her grief?

She looked at Dillon. His enthusiasm had dimmed, his eyes back to their familiar worried expression. She tried to smile at him. "Go ahead. Send him a text," she said. She didn't think it would do any good, but there was no harm in trying.

But he and Rose didn't get the chance.

The steady pounding of the rain outside had hidden the sound of a car pulling into the driveway, but the footsteps clattering up the stairs were unmistakable.

"Out of the way," Natalya snapped from the doorway to the room, Grace and Max right behind her. Natalya was carrying a device made of white plastic with a carrying handle, colorful buttons, and intricate displays.

Suddenly the already crowded room was overflowing, with ghosts and people brushing past and through one another. Nat stood directly on top of Rose, who backed up, almost tripping over Dillon, before she bumped into Zane's mom, who was greedily absorbing the sight of her family, eyes roaming from one to the next, taking in everything, even as Max stepped through her and craned to see Akira's body. From her position on the bed, Akira watched, bemused by the chaos.

"Thank God," Zane groaned, leaning back.

"You should have called me!" Nat's voice held fury. "Damn it, Zane, what were you doing anyway?"

"Not me," he said. "If I'd known this would happen, I'd have locked her in my office."

"She said the house was dangerous," Max pointed out, as Natalya efficiently began examining Akira, feeling for a pulse, then pulling open her shirt.

Oh, God. Akira squeezed her eyes closed. She supposed it was petty of her to be worried about which bra she was wearing when she was probably dead, but she really wished she'd chosen a nice discreet white instead of the black lace with hot pink lining this morning.

"What are you doing here?" Zane asked. "How did you know?"

"I saw it," Natalya responded.

"But you don't . . ." Zane started.

"Yes," she snapped. "I try very hard to ignore my visions, and you make it very difficult, little brother. This is the second time this year. Now get out of the way!"

As Zane backed away, Natalya pulled the paddles out of the box, and Akira realized what she was carrying.

A portable defibrillator.

Hmm. Spirit energy could cause random electrical energy in her brain that led to seizures: could disorganized electrical impulses also disrupt a heartbeat? If being hit by the spirit energy was like being hit by lightning, then maybe it had caused a simple cardiac arrest. In that case, the problem with her body might not be an aneurysm at all.

"Clear," Natalya said. There was a hum of electrical charge in the air as the power built in the battery-operated machine and she placed the pads on Akira's skin. And then, zap.

Everything went dark.

Shit, that hurt.

Akira forced her eyelids up.

It was Natalya's blue eyes that were looking down at her, not Zane's, and she felt a momentary stab of disappointment before she realized that seeing anyone's eyes from this position was a good sign. Her body hurt like she'd just run a marathon and then followed it up by sitting for a six-hour lecture, every muscle stiff and sore, but nothing felt broken. And although her head didn't feel good, it wasn't excruciating.

Licking her lips, she whispered, "Zane?"

Nat sighed and then smiled as she pulled back and let Zane take her place.

Akira looked up at him, at the worry in his face.

"I couldn't do it," he said. "I couldn't hurt you. It was so . . . it was too . . ." He shook his head, and Akira could hear the guilt and despair in his voice.

"I love that you couldn't do it," she said, voice husky, reaching to caress his face, sliding her hand along his cheek, loving the feel of him. A rush of love poured through her, so intense that the rest of the words just flowed out with it. "I love you."

He reached for her, sliding his arm around her neck, lifting her up, until he could bury his face in her hair. For a few moments, they sat there like that, his arms wrapped around her, Akira relaxing into the warmth of his body, and then he pulled back to kiss her, taking her lips with an urgent ferocity that started Akira's pulse racing.

Her heart must be working again, she thought fuzzily, as she kissed him back, the same urgency in her, locking her arms around his neck, until he let go of her mouth long enough to breathlessly say, "I love you, too," before he started kissing her again.

"All right, you two, break it up." Natalya's voice was amused but firm. "We need to make sure there's no permanent damage. I want to get Akira to a hospital as quickly as possible."

"No hospitals." Akira broke free from Zane to say. That was the last thing she needed.

"No hospitals," Zane agreed. "Now that Mom and Dillon are

gone, how about no more ghosts at all? Ever?"

Akira looked over his shoulder. Grace, Natalya, and Max were standing behind him, smiling with relief, but Dillon, Rose, and Zane's mom were right there with them, beaming just as happily.

"Um, yeah," Akira said. "That might not work."

❧CHAPTER EIGHTEEN☙

Thanksgiving Day

Akira wasn't convinced that deep-frying a turkey counted as a traditional Thanksgiving dinner. And if she'd left the whole meal to Zane, they'd be eating stuffing from a box, cranberries from a can, and Mrs. Smith's frozen pumpkin pie. But as she gazed out the bedroom window at the men clustered around the propane tank, she couldn't help the smile that curved her lips.

This was their first family dinner in her place (their place, she corrected herself, with secret delight) and Rose was over the moon with happiness, fluttering from kitchen to yard and back again, trying to be everywhere at once, almost dancing with joy.

Akira still wasn't quite sure what to think of Rose's return. After the events of August, Zane's mom had stuck around long enough to talk to each of her children and her husband, conversations facilitated by Akira without the ghostly possession part. Then she'd gone through the opening or passageway or whatever it was, eager to explore whatever came next.

Rose and Dillon, though, were still here: Rose because she liked it, Dillon because Rose insisted that he'd see his own door when it was time for him to move on. According to Rose, Henry was back, too, but Akira hadn't seen any sign of him. He definitely wasn't watching Lucas and Zane poking at the turkey, the way Rose and Dillon were.

Akira had asked Rose to tell her more about the doors and what was on the other side of them, but apparently trying to describe any of it was like trying to describe the cloudy place: the right words didn't exist. In a moment of surprising perception, Rose had said that it was like a butterfly trying to tell a caterpillar about flying. Akira had thought about that, about trying to explain wind currents and air pressure and velocity to a creature that only knew how to inch its way along a solid surface, and dropped the subject.

She was still curious, but she knew she'd learn more eventually.

As Akira watched, Lucas pulled out his phone. He grinned at it, showed it to Zane, and then said something to Max. Dillon must have texted him, Akira thought. He'd been working on communicating via cell phone ever since he and Rose had almost managed the feat in August and he'd gotten pretty good at it. Not long texts, not yet, but he could send a few words at a time.

She wondered what he'd said, but Zane was lifting the bird out of the hot oil, and she realized that she shouldn't be standing here daydreaming, not when she still had jobs to do. The stuffing and sweet potatoes were warming in the oven, the pumpkin pies cooling on the counter, the cranberry sauce with pecans, dried apricots and bourbon from Rose's mother's recipe already on the set table, but the potatoes were waiting to be mashed and the dinner rolls weren't finished baking.

First, though, she needed to change her clothes. As she crossed to her closet, she looked down at the red wine staining the front of her dress with a frown. Accidents happened, of course, but it had almost seemed as if Natalya had deliberately knocked over her glass.

She thought back to Nat's arrival. She would swear that Nat's expression showed a flash of disappointment when she saw Akira at the door. Had Nat been expecting Zane? But Nat had never been anything but welcoming to Akira, and it wasn't as if she could have been surprised to see Akira here: they were having the holiday meal at her house, after all.

Their house, she corrected herself again. She glanced down at the ring on her finger. They hadn't set a wedding date yet. Or picked a place for the ceremony or made any decisions about the reception or the honeymoon or even started working on the guest list. But a late October heat wave had inspired Zane to give her an early wedding present: the deed to the house and a new air conditioner.

He claimed that he'd gotten a great deal because the house was haunted. Not that it mattered, but she didn't entirely believe him. If it hadn't bothered the owner that the house was haunted before, why would it upset him now?

Besides, the house wasn't really haunted anymore. Despite Rose's absolute certainty that Henry was back, Akira hadn't seen him, and the boys in the backyard weren't the type of ghosts that would disturb anyone. And Rose wasn't tied to the house anymore: she could come and go as she pleased. Not that she pleased much. Guests were an exciting treat to Rose, but she was a homebody at heart, perfectly happy as long as she had music and television and the occasional company to talk to.

Not so Dillon. Being torn away from his car by the ghostly vortex had snapped his tie to the Taurus. He could now go anywhere he pleased and he was thrilled to be able to travel. Akira suspected that after the holiday he might head off with Lucas. It'd be a little lonely for him unless he found other ghosts to talk to, but he was ready for some adventure, she thought.

With a sigh, Akira considered her clothing options. Living with Zane meant both of them had to make some compromises about food—he thought meat, dessert and carbs ought to be fixtures at meals, not the occasional treat—and she'd gained a little weight, so most of her dressier clothes were going to be uncomfortably tight. Her hand hovered over a cranberry-colored silk dress. Dry clean only, so she rarely wore it, but she supposed she could trust Nat not to spill wine on her again.

By the time she entered the kitchen, Grace was already mashing the potatoes. "How much butter do you put in, Akira? Nat says two tablespoons is plenty, I say the whole stick."

"Most of the time I just use milk." All right, what in the world was going on with Nat? Her smile at the sight of Akira in her new dress was filled with glee, and looked just like Zane's when he beat Lucas at pool for the first time. Should she ask, Akira wondered?

But then Zane appeared in the doorway, laden down with a deep golden bird, and the moment was gone in the chaos of turkey carving and final preparations.

In the dining room, Akira had put place settings three to a side of the table, leaving the ends of the table empty. The arrangement was a little unusual, but not for a house with ghosts. But before they all sat down, Zane asked if they needed another chair.

When she looked at him curiously, he raised his brows and said, "Henry?"

Smiling—she loved the way Zane remembered the ghosts, even though he couldn't see them—Akira glanced at Rose, who was almost bouncing in her seat with excitement.

"Oh, no, Henry's fine," Rose assured her, waving the suggestion away. "He doesn't need a chair. But it was sweet of Zane to think of him."

Akira relayed the message, and then ran her eyes over the table.

Had she remembered everything? Butter, salt and pepper, side plates, the rolls, serving utensils for all the dishes . . . .

Hmm. She counted. Yes, a wine glass was missing, the glass that ought to be at her place setting. She glanced at Natalya, who was looking back at her, eyes bright, and then slipped into her seat without comment.

Max said grace, they passed the food, the siblings chatted and bickered cheerfully, everyone ate, but Akira sat silently, brain ticking away, until Zane caught her attention. "Okay?" he asked her, looking a little worried.

She'd been quiet for too long, she realized, so she smiled at him as she nodded. They'd been busy, she'd been happy, she'd felt fine—oh, if she'd thought about it, she might have realized, but she hadn't been thinking.

She felt as if she was glowing with happiness, and maybe he saw it on her face, because he quirked a brow at her. She just smiled a little wider, and turned her head to Natalya, who was sitting next to him.

"Is this the right dress?" she asked Nat. No one else at the table understood the question, but Natalya pressed her lips together instead of answering. Akira could see the smile in her eyes, though. "It was a two-year contract," Akira continued. "So you knew what you'd seen was on Thanksgiving, but thought maybe this Thanksgiving was too soon?"

Natalya still didn't say anything, but Max was looking curious and Grace and Lucas had paused in their conversation about some complaint filed with the SEC about General Directions that might or might not be going to cause another investigation into their business practices.

Akira stood. She felt as if the happiness was going to explode out of her and she wanted to be next to Zane, touching him, when it did. Walking around the table, she paused by Rose's chair. "Henry's comfortable where he is?" she asked.

"Very," Rose replied cheerfully. "He won't remember later, but we can remind him."

Akira nodded, and continued around the table. Nat wasn't even trying to hide her smile, but everyone else looked mystified. When she got to Zane, Akira held out her hand, and he stood, taking her hand with his.

"We need to decide on a wedding date," she told him, loving his perplexed expression, the confusion in his blue eyes.

"Okay," he answered obligingly. "June or October?" Those were the dates they'd been talking about: June for the tradition, October because it was the nicest time of year in central Florida.

Akira shook her head. "I was thinking more like next weekend. We're going to be much too busy in June."

She waited for him to realize what she meant, but when he didn't get it fast enough, she pulled his hand to her and placed it on her stomach, and as Zane realized what she was saying, his face lit up, and he wrapped his arms around her, lifting her off her feet with exuberant joy.

All she'd been looking for when she came to Tassamara was a place where she could exist, where she could survive unnoticed. Instead, she'd found everything she'd ever wanted.

A home.

Love.

Safety.

And a family.

❧TO MY READERS☙

If you're an active reviewer and want a free review copy of either the next book in the series or the next book I release, please send an email to reviews@sarahwynde.com with a link to a review you've written about one of my books, and let me know which title you'd like to receive and in what format (epub, mobi, or pdf).

The review can be on any site, including a retailer, Goodreads, LibraryThing, Shelfari, your personal blog or a group blog, and it definitely doesn't have to be nice. Be as critical as you like, but please write at least a few sentences—two-word reviews don't count!

If you'd like to know when I'm releasing a new book or get an occasional free short story or missing scene in your inbox, sign up for my mailing list at sarahwynde.com/find-me/.

You can also email me at sarah@sarahwynde.com or find me on Facebook as Sarah Wynde or on Twitter as Wyndes. Or you can find me on one of my blogs. Wynded Words at sarahwynde.com is my home site, and The Write Push at writepush.wordpress.com is a group blog where I and a couple of other authors post about our progress and our thoughts on what we're learning. On tumblr, I'm at wyndes.tumblr.com.

Best wishes and thanks for reading!

Sarah

~OTHER WORKS~

A Gift of Thought

Sylvie swore she'd never go back to Tassamara. She was wrong.

At seventeen, Sylvie Blair left her infant son with his grandparents while she went shopping. She never returned. Twenty years later, she's devastated to learn of his early, untimely death. But although Dillon's body is long since buried, his spirit lingers on.

And he's not real happy.

He doesn't like his mom's job—too dangerous. He doesn't like her apartment—too boring. And he definitely doesn't like her love life—non-existent.

But when Dillon decides that his parents should be living happily ever after, he sets them on a path that leads deeper and deeper into danger.

Can Sylvie let go of the past and embrace the future?

And can Dillon survive the deadly energy he unwittingly unleashes?

The Spirits of Christmas (A Tassamara Short Story)

Akira's plans are simple: write wedding invitations, bake Christmas cookies, and eat red meat. (The last surprises her, too.) But when Rose, the ghost who haunts her house, asks for a favor, Akira can't say no. Although she's faced danger before, even death, a toddler who doesn't like peanut-butter-and-jelly might be her worst nightmare.

□

A Gift of Time

She thought she could see everything. Time is proving her wrong.

Ten years ago, Natalya's ability to remember the future cost her the life she wanted when her vision of her fiancé's death tore them apart. Ever since, she's considered her precognition more of a curse than a gift. How can she live in the present when the future looms so large?

But when the night she's long dreaded finally arrives, Natalya's vision and reality diverge. She and her ex, Colin, are drawn into a web of the unexplained, led by a mysterious little girl. Who is Kenzi? And where did she come from? The little girl might be the reason Fate has spared Colin's life, but could she also bring Natalya and Colin together again?

With Colin, Kenzi, her family, the townspeople of Tassamara, and a set of circumstances that nobody could foresee, Natalya must solve the puzzle of a lifetime. Her discovery that her gift is not the only one at work will change the lives of everyone around her as time becomes precious in a most unexpected way… and the clock is ticking.

A Lonely Magic (Coming June 2014)

Fen, a street-smart, 21-year-old orphan with anxiety issues, thinks she has her life under control until a gorgeous stranger tries to kill her and a mysterious boy comes to her rescue. Now she's caught up in the adventure of a lifetime, one that will take her from the cold streets of Chicago to the glorious blue waters of the Caribbean, and into a world she never imagined existed.

□

ACKNOWLEDGEMENTS

You know how some authors say that they always wanted to write? That they've been scribbling in notebooks their whole life? That it was everything they'd ever dreamed about?

I am not one of them.

Oh, sure, every few years I'd try to write. I love to read and I'm a compulsive daydreamer, so writing is a natural fit. Unfortunately, I'm also tough on myself. I wrote, I read, I hated, I ripped up (and then later, hit delete). And after each failed attempt, I wouldn't write for years.

Then I discovered fan fiction. And with it, an audience of wonderful, supportive, enthusiastic fellow writers and readers. I wrote about a quarter of a million words of fan fiction before turning to original fiction, and received well over a thousand reviews. I'm not going to list the name of every person who wrote a review (admit it, you'd stop reading!), but I did want to take this opportunity to say thank you: thank you, thank you, thank you, to everyone who ever reviewed my fics—you gave me the courage to believe in my stories, even when I was sure the words weren't doing the story justice.

Thank you, more specifically, to Allyrien aka Rachel (my chapters don't feel real until you tell me what you think of them); to Sara aka Justine (you give me faith that my words work in my most doubting moments); and to Zero aka Tim (a parenthetical is not nearly enough room to appreciate your endless patience and willingness to consult on tone and structure, punctuation and male psychology.)

When I started writing original fiction, I posted chapters to fictionpress.com. Leaving my lovely little fan community for the world of original fiction was a lot like being kicked out of a nest (although I suppose I jumped, really), and I want to thank everyone who reviewed A Gift of Ghosts while it was in progress. So thank you, so much, to Everis, Nereemac, JMill, DonHanz, Amy, Kat, Shayna-18, Kaypgirl, AlternateShadesofBlue, RyaJynx, Darlove99, Lorina Lee Belmont218, Heather, Ann Barthel, Hoshi14, Magz,

Miisu, World of Ink, Purplelover, Luckycool9, Ahrendaaria, FamishedNight, Bittie752, Far Wanderer, Cat Parmegiani, Ruki44, Bird That Flies At Dawn, Hatondog, Lonnee, and Shineyma. Your encouragement kept me going.

I also posted chapters to Critique Circle. I need to say first of all that every adverb, every use of the word "was," and every misplaced comma are mine, all mine, and the people who generously critiqued my work bear no responsibility for the above. That said, I'd like to thank MikeKent, MimiWriter, Harleyquin, Katamuki, LornaB, Jaylia, Mpolish, KSullivan, Baker, Egryphon, and Wim for their insight and feedback.

Jaime Norwood's comments were exactly what I needed to hear: whether it was point of view issues or doubts about tone, Jaime, your concrete, insightful assistance made this a better book. Christine Pearson, your character analysis helped me enormously, and Maggie Sharp (the world's nicest sister-in-law!), your questions made for some great last-minute tweaks. Thank you all so much!

Finally, I want to thank my sister, Karen Lowery, for reading what I write and telling me I'm wonderful. Our mom asked me once why I'd never given her anything of mine to read, and I told her it was because I already knew she would read it and tell me it was wonderful and that she loved it and that she was proud of me, and so I was okay with letting her skip the actual reading part. I didn't let my sister skip the actual reading part, but I still appreciate the unconditional support she gives me. Thanks, Karen!